Praise for the Mage Wars card game!

Mage Wars is "the 2nd Best Game O̶F̶ ̶A̶"
– Tom Vasel, Dice Tower

"...makes for a complex dynamic an͜
– Kaja Sadowski, Starlit Citadel.

"...a game that is designed really, really well."
– Joanna Gaskell, Starlit Citadel.

2013 ORIGINS BEST BOARD GAME NOMINEE!
"No game I've ever played so aptly communicates the imaginative vision
of two dueling casters, each pulling out all the stops to hold off their foe."
– Matt Miller, Game Informer

**MAGE WARS IS NOW IN THE TOP 25 GAMES
ON BOARD GAME GEEK!**
Out of tens of thousands of games we're ranked #25 and climbing!
2,800+ ratings - 8.29 overall score!
– Board Game Geek

#1 BEST OVERALL TWO-PLAYER GAME
Mage Wars® is "above and beyond everything!" It "can't be oversold... how
good this game is." Mage Wars® has "very thematic effects that make
sense."
– Joel Eddy, Drive Thru Reviews

2013 GAME OF THE YEAR – 3CON
Mage Wars® wins Game of the Year at 3Con in Fort Wayne, IN.
"Since I made my Best Games of 2012 list, none of them still has come
close to topping Mage Wars!"
– Tom Vasel, Forcemaster vs. Warlord Review, Dice Tower

"Mage Wars creates a stunning sense of epic moments...making you feel
like a bad-ass mage of incredible power. I truly love Mage Wars...it just has
it all!"
– David Sterling, Giant Fire Breathing Robot.

"Dueling mages...Mage Wars pulls it off with so much style and attention
to detail!...There really is nothing else quite like it!" Ranked 9.4 out of 10.
**– Junjun Gonzaga, Board Game Geek review
Best Card Game 2012! - SpieLama.de Boardgame Awards**

"For this amazing achievement and its combination of tactical and strategic elements the KartenSpieLama Award 2012 goes to MAGE WARS!"
– Benjamin Schönheiter, Editor-in-Chief

"Best game of 2012 – The ONE game to rule them all! Amazing Depth and Playability! You must play this game – you owe it to yourself!"
– Scott Fera, SuperRad Dad, in Top games of 2012 Podcast

"Best Game of 2012! – Mage Wars is by far, the most fresh, fun, exhilarating time I've had sitting across from an opponent in years, let alone through all of 2012! Mage Wars is a beautiful work of art!"
– Scott "Tox" Morris, Crits Happen

"Best Game of 2012, by far! I foresee great things for this game in the future!"
– Tom Vasel, Dice Tower

MAGE WARS #1 CUSTOMIZABLE CARD GAME FOR 2012!
"Super innovative!…sucks you right in!"
– Joel Eddy, Drive Thru Review

IN THE TOP 5 GAMES OF 2012!
"Mage Wars offered some of the most rewarding gameplay of 2012"
– Michael Barnes, No High Scores

ONE OF THE 10 BEST GAMES OF 2012.
"Mage Wars®…revels in marvelous complexity!"
– Jesse Dean, 10 Best Games of 2012, Board Game Geek

"From the two of us, it is a go get! Yes, absolutely."
– R Jay McCarty and Nick Bock, Duel Review #438 - Mage Wars, Duel Reviews

"It lives up to the hype and surpasses all of my expectations! Mage Wars is a game of layers that rewards you each time you dig a bit deeper."
– Cyrus Kirby, Editor in Chief, Father Geek

"This game has it ALL: strategy, polish and a whole lot of flavor …I can't stop playing! I rate it a 9.5"
– Benjamin Schönheiter, Editor-in-Chief, SpieLama.de

"This is a power gamer's dream!"
– Jim Wittwer, BoardGaming.com

"This game RULES, and is one of the best games we have ever played!"
"Mage Wars is the dream comes true for every player."
– Dusan Vit, editor for Deskovehry.com

"I give this the highest rating possible for a game!"
– Sam Healey, Dice Tower

"This game is one of my favorite games…It replaces Magic the Gathering for me."
– Tom Vasel

"This game is friggin' amazing!…It crushes Summoner Wars, Dungeon Command, and Magic!."
– Joel Eddy, Drive Thru Review

"Fantastic components! …Fantastic depth! …I love this game! Could not come more highly recommended!"
– Scott Fera, SuperRad Dad

"Great detailed tactical game play experience…incredible versatility…near endless replay value!"
– Enrico Nardini, Editor in Chief, Play Unplugged

"This game gets the biggest Crit I could give one!"
– Scott "Tox" Morris, Crits Happen

"Mage Wars is our new favorite game and possibly the best game of the year!"
– Table Talk Games

"Mage Wars scores 9.0 - 9.5 on the components alone!"
– MadShepard

"Great game!…Awesome!"
– Cat and Mouse

MAGE WARS®

The Nature of the Beast
WILL McDERMOTT

Edited by Hannah Elder
Cover art by Craig Spearing
Book design by Jason Ullmeyer

Arcane Wonders
Dallas, TX
United States of America
arcanewonders.com

Dynamite Entertainment
113 Gaither Dr., Ste. 205
Mt. Laurel, NJ 08054
dynamite.com

For Dynamite:
Nick Barrucci, CEO / Publisher
Juan Collado, President / COO
Rich Young, Director Business Development
Keith Davidsen, Marketing Manager

Joe Rybandt, Senior Editor
Hannah Elder, Associate Editor
Molly Mahan, Associate Editor

Jason Ullmeyer, Design Director
Katie Hidalgo, Graphic Designer
Chris Caniano, Digital Associate
Rachel Kilbury, Digital Assistant

ISBN: 978-1-60690-573-9

Publisher's Cataloging-in-Publication data
Prepared by Adrienne Bashista

McDermott, Will.
    Mage wars : nature of the beast / by Will McDermott.
    p. cm.
    ISBN 978-1-60690-571-5 (ebook)
    ISBN 978-1-60690-572-2 (POD)
    ISBN 978-1-60690-573-9 (pbk.)

1. Elves --Fiction. 2. Magic --Fiction. 3. Dwarfs --Fiction. 4. Adventure Fiction.
5. Fantasy fiction. I. Title.

PS3613.C386945 .M34 2014
813.6 --dc23

First printing March 2015
Printed in Canada

This book is dedicated to my loyal first reader and wonderful daughter, Elyse, for all of her help and support during the writing of this book. Sorry I kept making you cry during the sad parts.

PROLOGUE: DWARVEN ARENA

"I demand trial by combat," declared Digur. The dwarven Forcemaster swiped pudgy fingers through his close-cropped, dirt-brown hair and then used the back of his hand to wipe the sweat from his brow. He hoped the crowd that had gathered in the arena hadn't noticed the quaver in his voice.

He had wanted to sound forceful and confidant when he demanded his right to defend his views on the battlefield. However, his voice had sounded weak and small in the enormous, underground chamber that doubled as both court and arena for the Anvil Throne dwarves.

The rectangular chamber was exactly 120 meters long by 90 meters wide and 40 meters high. The walls ran straight and true, forming perfect 90-degree angles at every corner. The arena was a marvel of dwarven magic and engineering, as Digur should know. He had helped construct it.

Flickering light from hundreds of torches held in sconces at regular intervals along the walls did little to illuminate the vastness of the chamber, and created strange shadows that danced across the intricately etched floor.

Digur had designed the pattern on the floor. It appeared random to the untrained eye, but actually repeated across the stone floor of the arena, making the floor appear as if it had been inlaid with thousands of cobblestones. However, Digur had never noticed the eeriness of the light as it moved across the pattern until he'd been forced to stand, alone, in the middle of the dancing shadows.

Forcing his eyes away from the flickering floor, Digur scanned the crowd. Halfway up each wall, large windows bordered by thick, stone pillars opened into viewing chambers. Spectators sat on long steps carved out of bare rock and watched the spectacle below. The side viewing chambers were packed to capacity as row upon row of angry dwarves stared down at Digur.

A few in the crowd clapped when Digur called for trial by combat, but they stopped quickly under the glare of the ministers, who sat at a long table in the middle of the rear viewing chamber. These nine elder dwarves wearing supple leather, fine furs, and bright, gold adornments would decide his fate, although Digur knew that only one vote on the council truly mattered.

Much of the crowd jeered at Digur. Perhaps they had tired of his near-constant disruption to their lives over the past few months. Or, perhaps the ministers had simply done a remarkable job of painting him as the face of evil that threatened their way of life.

By far, though, the majority of the crowd leaned forward on the steps with huge grins plastered on their mostly bearded faces. It was obvious to Digur this crowd was eager to see the spectacle of an arena battle.

So much for his short-lived career as a leader of the movement, he thought. All he had accomplished by speaking out against his kin's long-standing policy of isolationism was a quick trial and a battle he had little chance of winning. Either way, his ultimate fate was sealed, and he knew it.

Minister Grimhammer, a dour old dwarf with a face that could chisel granite and a temper that could turn rock into magma, sat in the middle of the ministers. All eyes eventually turned to watch her, and while she didn't smile, she drank in the attention like a vampire sucks blood.

The golden medallion of office that hung around her neck jangled noisily as she raised the stone of judgment from the table in front of her and banged it down on the table. The crack of stone striking against stone reverberated throughout the arena.

The crowd hushed immediately, not just out of tradition, but also out of a respect that bordered on fear for the minister. King Bellowspark may rule the Anvil Throne, but Minister Grimhammer, the de facto leader of the council of elders, made sure the kingdom ran smoothly, like a well-oiled dwarven war-machine.

"Request granted!" she said. "Digur Diamondust, you will face the champion of the Anvil Throne in the arena. Should you be defeated, you will be sentenced immediately for your crimes of sedition, sowing discord within the kingdom of the Anvil Throne, and treason against the monarchy. You will then be banished to the farthest reaches of the realm."

The minister stared at him down her long, hawkish nose, and banged the stone onto the table again. "You will live out your days tending the Temple of the Twelve Diamonds, where you will have no interaction with the rest of dwarven society."

The stone slammed down once again, and Digur felt the impact all the way down to his stomach.

*   *   *   *   *   *

Digur stood in one corner of the giant, underground arena. The great stone walls he'd help cut out of the mountain towered above him, while the torches provided just enough light to see his opponent as a dim shadow in the other corner, more than a hundred meters away.

Digur didn't need to see the Grax to know it was him, though. He'd seen Graxdonis Rockgrinder fight dozens of duels in the arena and the Warlord had never lost a battle. Over the years, he'd come to be known simply as "the Grax," which meant "the Greatest."

He was a mountain of a dwarf. He stood almost two meters tall and was a full meter wide at the shoulders. Flowing blond hair framed his chiseled face and draped across the high-stacked armor plates covering his shoulders. He kept his blond beard cropped short, though, perhaps to show off his jutting chin, which was always limned in an eerie light from the glowing runes etched into his harshforge armor.

On his back, the Grax wore a massive, jade-headed hammer set on a silver shaft that had been inlaid with magical runes. On his head he wore a double-horned helm with a red plume of roc tail feathers that created a red stripe through his blond hair as it cascaded down his back.

Digur took a deep breath as he waited for the bang of the stone of judgment, which would begin the duel. He had a plan. The Grax won every battle the same way, by controlling the arena with conjurations long enough that he could summon huge, unstoppable creatures. Digur just needed to hit him fast and keep him off balance. Simple.

The stone rang out a sharp tone and Digur focused the energy in his mind and began channeling mana between his palms. A moment later, a glowing blob of protoplasm appeared in the air above him. Two bulging eyes protruded from the bottom of the blob while tendrils of energy arced across the bulbous protrusions above.

Digur started at the thoughtspore and allowed the creature to reach into his mind to grab a spell. Crimson plasma flowed from Digur's forehead and snaked its way up toward the thoughtspore. It coalesced around a needle-like appendage that hung from the bottom of the blob and formed into the shape of a giant hammer.

Satisfied with his initial work, Digur glanced across the arena to see what the Grax had done. As usual, the dwarven champion had conjured a construction yard and then sprinted toward the middle of the arena while the enormous conjuration came into being behind him.

With his mind, Digur sent his thoughtspore off toward the middle of the arena as well. He then channeled a ball of magic into one palm, reached into the energy ball, and pulled out a double-edged force blade.

With his blade in hand, Digur strode toward the Grax, trying to exude more confidence than he truly felt inside. The Grax had already conjured barracks that would soon begin pumping out soldiers, while the dwarven champion ran toward the back corner of the arena.

Of course, that was exactly where Digur knew he would head, and exactly where he wanted him. Perhaps this really could work.

Digur sent his thoughtspore around the barracks and on toward the construction yard. He then began channeling crimson energy into his palm, intending to move closer to his opponent and attack him with an invisible fist before entering melee range.

However, the Grax must have anticipated the Forcemaster's attack because he moved out of range before Digur could advance. The dwarven champion took several steps back toward the construction yard before conjuring a tall, wooden armory in the corner of the arena where he had been standing just moments before.

Undeterred, Digur moved forward and cast his invisible fist on top of the armory, knocking several logs off the top of the conjured building, which dissipated into green energy as they fell toward the arena floor.

Digur then turned and gathered some mana of his own. After muttering a single word, he hurled the energy up into the air, where it exploded into an electro-statically charged orb. Digur hoped his suppression orb would slow down the Grax's imminent army of soldiers long enough for him to complete his plan.

Digur moved next to the armory to get close enough to enact his plan. However, before Digur could do anything, he heard a noise from the barracks. He looked over to see a stooped, green-skinned creature appear. The goblin wore bulbous goggles and carried a pack full of tools.

The Grax was right where he needed him, but he had to act fast. Soon the barracks would overwhelm him with soldiers that would all be well equipped with extra armor and pointy weapons from the Warlord's conjured armory.

Digur steeled his determination, moved in front of the armory, and prepared to spring his little trap. He recited a quick incantation, gathering blue energy between his palms and then thrust both arms toward the Grax.

Bluish tendrils of energy shot out toward the Warlord, slamming into his chest and pushing him back toward the construction yard.

Unfazed by his sudden shift in location, the Grax just smiled and then calmly charged his horned helm with a command spell, before gathering a double-handful of verdant-green mana, which he tossed back toward the spot where he'd been standing before the force push.

In a moment, an altar began to take shape out of the green miasma. Great stone stairs led to a raised platform bordered at the corners by tapering stone pillars topped by half-meter-long stone finials. On top of the platform, the mana coalesced into a giant statue of an imposing man gesturing toward the horizon, his cape fluttering in an unseen wind, his other hand holding a huge halberd on a two-and-a-half-meter-tall pike. It was Talos, the legendary servant of the gods of war.

The entire artifact stood over ten meters tall and struck terror into anyone who had ever seen this altar dominate a duel if allowed to charge up to full power. Digur had to hope his plan could prevent that from happening.

"Time to wipe that smile off your face," said Digur, half to himself to bolster his courage, and half to the gathered audience. No matter what, he wanted everyone to know that he had faced the dwarven champion with courage.

Digur quickly gathered mossy-green mana in his hand, and then channeled even more energy from his body into the spell. This would take almost every ounce of power he had at the moment, but the results should be worth it.

The Forcemaster extended both arms away from his body and sprayed the mossy mana toward his opponent. Instead of hitting him with it, though, Digur used the energy to construct a wall of stone between himself and the Warlord. However, he wasn't done once the final stone formed out of the mist. The Forcemaster extended the mana around the corner and began forming a second wall perpendicular to the first, penning the Grax in the corner of the arena with his construction yard.

Digur was so happy that he'd sprung his trap and successfully walled the Warlord into a corner that he almost forgot to have his thoughtspore attack. However, instead of attacking the Grax, he commanded it to fling the force hammer at the construction yard. He needed to tear down the champion's outposts before the altar of domination came to life.

The thoughtspore's hammer flew over the stone wall and slammed into the construction yard, almost completely demolishing the wheel-powered crane in the middle of the yard. Digur let out a giddy little laugh. One more hit like that and the construction yard would disappear back into the ether. This was really working!

With the Warlord walled off in a corner, Digur could turn his attention back to destroying the outposts. Pulsing tendrils of mana already emanated from the tops of all three outposts, reaching out to one another to create a triangle of energy that fed into the altar of domination. He had to break that connection, but before he could even swing his force blade, Digur saw the Grax's hammer fly up over the wall and slam into his thoughtspore.

The hammer struck the amorphous creature right between its bulging eyes, tore through its protoplasm body and exited through the top of the blob, and then returned, disappearing behind the wall.

Energy spewed from the top and bottom of the thoughtspore like blood gushing from open wounds for a few moments before the creature simply dissolved into nothingness.

Digur sighed, but knew he would need to summon more creatures eventually. However, he wasn't prepared for what happened next.

Almost an instant after the jade-headed hammer returned to Grax, the Warlord slammed it right through the stone wall. Rocks and bits of mortar flew away from the giant dwarf in every direction, raining down on the ground by the altar, where it all dissolved away into a green mist.

Astounded by how quickly the Grax had destroyed both his main attacker and the wall of his cage, Digur despaired. He now had to destroy the armory. He turned and swung his force blade, cutting a neat hole in the wooden log wall, but knew he would need some stronger attack spells to bring it down quickly.

A movement at his side made Digur glance over at the barracks, where he saw that a little friend had joined the goblin. The two goblin builders looked at one another briefly before the first one trotted toward Digur. He was surprised by the speed of the creature, considering it ran just like it did everything else—practically doubled over at the waist. In a moment, it stood between Digur and the armory.

As Digur wracked his brain for some way to destroy the armory before the goblins repaired all the damage, he heard a thrumming sound coming from the altar. He looked over and saw that statue of Talos had begun to glow. He didn't like the look of that at all. Worse yet, another soldier had popped out of the barracks; not a goblin this time, though, but an Anvil Throne dwarf holding a crossbow.

The sight of a third enemy creature appearing on the arena floor when Digur had none made him panic. Instead of staying on the offensive, he decided to go completely defensive, hoping to hold out long enough to destroy the armory. In quick succession, he cast a spell to charm the Anvil Throne crossbowman and then placed a forcefield enchantment around himself.

Unfortunately, he probably squandered his one chance to bring down the armory. The goblin standing between him and the conjured outpost took up a guarding position, while the other goblin ran over to begin repairing the structure.

At the same time, the Grax moved up next to the glowing altar, spun his hammer over his head and flung it at Digur. It glanced off the forcefield and returned to the Warlord.

As the glow around the statue grew brighter, Digur saw the barracks deploy another Anvil Throne crossbowman. However, the goblins were the bigger problem. He gathered some energy and spread his hands out to either side of him, casting wave after wave of blue energy out from his body.

The energy waves repulsed the goblins, sending them flying off in either direction from the armory. With the way clear, Digur slashed his force blade at the wooden wall once more. He hoped beyond hope that he had enough force behind the blow to finally sunder the wall and bring the outpost crashing down in a heap of dissolving energy.

Luck was not with Digur, however. His mighty slash cut through most of the timbers in the wall, but left the corner supports intact. The armory creaked and swayed but ultimately remained standing.

Moments later, both goblins returned. One took position to guard the structure while the other began repairs. The Grax strode up right behind the goblins. He activated the spell in his helm and took two mighty swipes at the Forcemaster with his jade-headed hammer.

Both attacks glanced harmlessly off Digur's forcefield, but he knew this was a losing proposition. The shield enchantment needed time to regenerate fully between blows, and another flurry like that would rip through it and leave him defenseless.

Behind the Grax, glowing cracks began to spider web across the statue of Talos as if the power growing inside the altar could no longer be contained and sought to escape into the arena. Time was running out for Digur and he knew it. He needed to destroy the armory now or the altar would activate.

He ignored the goblins and prepared a single spell, gathering crimson energy into the palm of one hand. He concentrated on the ball of mana and uttered a command word that made the energy in his hand bubble up and flow like lava, growing and solidifying into a rock as he watched.

When the ever-growing ball of hardening magma reached the size of a cannonball, he threw it over the head of the guarding goblin, straight at the armory. The rock grew as it flew through the air, becoming a huge boulder that fell out of the air and crushed the armory flat.

Digur shouted in triumph as his boulder and the smashed bits of armory dissolved back into their respective clouds of mana, creating a brown puddle of gasses on the arena floor that slowly dissipated.

More importantly, the triangle of energy beams connecting the three outposts that had been funneling mana into the statue of Talos, winked out. The statue still glowed through a myriad of cracks interlacing its entire surface, but it could not activate now—not without a third outpost powering it.

However, this moment of triumph was short-lived. The Grax simply smiled at his much smaller opponent as he gathered two handfuls of mossy green mana in his hands and uttered a new conjuration spell.

Where the armory had dissolved away into nothingness moments before, a new, stone outpost began to form. Sharpened logs jutted out from the base of the six-meter-tall garrison platform. Long wooden posts at each corner, protected by additional sharpened spikes, supported a peaked frame covered by thin sheets of leather that stretched tight at the corners.

Above the garrison, tendrils of mana snaked out toward the other two outposts. Once the energy triangle formed again, it began pulsing mana toward the altar. Digur was doomed.

To punctuate his imminent defeat, Digur felt a crossbow bolt ping off his forcefield from behind. He glanced back toward the barracks and saw the second crossbowman begin reloading his weapon. Next to him stood a new goblin, who was fumbling with a sling.

Deciding to go down with a fight, Digur turned toward the Grax and swung his force blade at the dwarven champion. His energy blade slashed across the Warlord's armor, cutting a slice through the plates and drawing blood, but did little real damage. It was a small victory at best. Digur had seen many fine mages defeated by the Grax without landing a single hit.

The Grax smiled and swung his hammer over his head. The breeze of the spinning hammer made the Warlord's flaxen hair sway around his face. He then slammed the hammer down at Digur, landing a mighty blow that nearly sent Digur sprawling—more from the surprise than the actual damage. His forcefield no longer protected him.

As the two goblins took up guarding positions in front of the garrison, Digur glanced around the arena. The Grax had two ranged attackers plinking away at him from the barracks. He had two goblins standing in his way and preventing him from attacking the Grax or the Garrison, and the altar was practically thrumming with energy.

He should simply concede, but he had decided to see this battle through to the end. Before all of this, no one in the Anvil Throne had known Digur from a hole in the mountain. No one would care if he lived or died today. He had no family left and no legacy to protect. He might as well disappear for all the impact he had had on the world.

But he had stood up for something he believed in. He had spoken out against how the ministers were handling the rock devil problem; how they were sticking their heads in a steam vent and hoping the problem would simply bury itself under the weight of the mountain. And, he was damned if he would let them get the satisfaction of seeing him quit.

He prepared a couple of spells for the coming onslaught and dug in his heels. A moment later, the altar exploded with a blinding white light. Shards of stone flew in every direction and turned back into a cloud of mana as they scattered throughout the arena.

As the light dimmed back to normal, it looked for a moment like the statue of Talos still stood where the altar had once been, but then Digur saw the statue move! It turned toward Digur and brought its great halberd swinging around to grab it in both hands. Talos had come to life!

Digur cast a quick enchantment on himself and then, as the golden glow of the first enchantment encircled his body, he began casting another spell, directed at Talos. A giant blue hand reached out from Digur and tried to encircle the statuesque Talos. When the ethereal hand tried to crush the summoned servant of the gods of war, Talos simply stepped through the blue fingers and advanced on the diminutive Forcemaster.

Digur was grateful for the protection of his forcefield and the other enchantment he had placed on himself. However, before Talos arrived, he felt a projectile impact him from behind. He didn't want his new enchantment to activate yet, so he willed the forcefield to use its last charge to deflect the crossbow bolt.

Unfortunately, after the crossbow bolt caromed off Digur's forcefield, he felt the ping of a sling bullet hit his shoulder, which activated the enchantment. A new, blue energy field flared up between Digur and the sling bullet. The bullet ricocheted off the field and traveled in a straight line back toward the goblin slinger, smacking the green creature in the gut. Blood boiled up through the hole left by the bullet's passing and the goblin screamed.

Completely unprotected, Digur held his force blade up in front of himself defensively, waiting for the next two attacks.

The Grax swung his hammer and Digur used his innate telekinetic powers to parry it aside. The blow was so forceful that the hammer still glanced off his shoulder, nearly dislocating his arm. Unfortunately, he could only use that trick once, and his force blade would be of no use to the follow-up attack Digur knew was coming.

Fueled by battle fury, the Grax used the momentum of his first hammer attack to swing around for another blow. This one hit Digur squarely in the temple, making his ears ring and blurring his sight.

The arena grew dim and fuzzy around him. He blinked a couple of times to clear his vision, if not his head. When he could see again, it was just in time to see a giant axe head on the end of a two-and-a-half-meter-long halberd coming at him!

Talos's aim was true and the halberd sliced through Digur's robes, cutting into his torso just below his ribs. The Forcemaster screamed as the axe blade sliced him nearly in half. He looked down to see blood and guts begin oozing out of the long slash across his midsection. A moment later, unconsciousness enveloped Digur's brain, graciously removing him from the arena, the duel, and the excruciating pain of that final attack.

CHAPTER 1: FIGHT AND FLIGHT

High above the edge of the Straywood, where the dark-green tree line of the forest met the gray and beige foothills of the Anvil Throne, a lone falcon soared. Ever on the verge of a stall, the Thunderift falcon, who was named Artemis by the wood elf prowling the forest's edge below, stretched his cloud-white wings to their fullest, spread gold-tipped pin feathers out to grab every shred of lift, and glided above the verdant treetops and sun-drenched scrubland.

White wisps of clouds strewn across the bright azure sky above Artemis barely diminished the sun's power as the falcon flew in slow circles, basking in its rays. Below him, his keen falcon eyes caught every movement in the trees, every flicker of life amongst the lowland's scrub and rocks, every potential prey, and every possible danger to his master.

Artemis beat his wings once and then again to prevent the inevitable stall as he looped around in another long arc across the sky. To the north, past the snow-covered peaks of the Anvil Throne, he could just spy the coastline of the Diamond Sea. To the east, the dwarven mountain range extended as far as even his eyes could see. To the south and west, cutting a vicious scar across the southern edge of his master's lush, verdant forest, lay the Darkfenne, a foul place full of muck and sour-tasting vermin.

Artemis enjoyed patrolling the northeastern edge of the great forest. The moles and chipmunks that skittered to and fro in the foothills below were tender and fast, providing both a challenge and a tasty meal. Plus, the days here meandered one into another, with little excitement ever intruding on his lazy, thermal-fueled circles.

A gentle tug in the forefront of Artemis's small brain snapped his attention back to his task. He peered down at the scrubs and rocks of the foothills, scanning for any movement larger than a mole. After noting a couple of potential midday meal opportunities but no other creatures, he scanned the tree line, once again seeking any indication of danger to either the forest or his master.

Seeing nothing, not even his wood elf master—such was the skill of this Beastmaster that he could hide from even the keen eyes of a Thunderift falcon—Artemis flapped his great wings once more, thinking to resume his mindless circling, while planning a diving attack on the fat mole he had just spied.

At that moment, Artemis noticed a rustling of leaves at the edge of the forest, south of where he'd last seen his master. He constricted his pinfeathers, pulled in his wings slightly, and altered the angle of his tail feathers to begin descending and narrow his circle over the location of the movement. There. He saw it again. Two distinct sets of leaves rustled almost simultaneously, one within the underbrush and the other in the vines hanging down from the canopy.

Artemis drew in a deep breath and screeched. At the same moment, he folded his wings into his body, tilted his tail feathers down toward his legs, and dove toward the forest floor.

*　　*　　*　　*　　*　　*

Jhonart glanced up through the foliage when he heard Artemis screech. After only a second he found his pet, a white streak against the bright sky, dropping like an arrow, straight and true.

The tall wood elf stepped back from the edge of the forest, his large frame barely disturbing a single leaf, his leather-clad feet making no sound and leaving little trace of his passing on the moss-covered forest floor.

Jhonart turned south and picked his way through the undergrowth, using his falcon-topped staff to push bushes and low-hanging limbs soundlessly out of the way. He moved far faster and more gracefully than a two-meter-tall, 14-stone person person had any right to move.

Artemis screeched again, indicating he had found his prey. Jhonart closed his eyes for a moment and concentrated to strengthen the bond between Beastmaster and pet. When he opened his eyes again, Jhonart saw not the forest in front of him, but the patch of ground beneath Artemis, who had come to rest on a branch above a small clearing.

Jhonart sighed and dismissed the pet's vision before continuing his trek through the undergrowth. A moment later he came out of the trees into the small clearing. With a flutter of wings, Artemis dropped out of the tree and flapped over to land on the fur-lined shoulders of Jhonart's bearskin jerkin.

The beating of wings seemed to startle the other figure in the clearing who turned to face Jhonart, a smile spreading across her face.

"Greetings, Jhonart," said the female elf. "You look well today. Quite healthy, indeed, actually." Her smile broadened across her almond-shaped face, the corners of her mouth practically disappearing behind her cascading raven tresses.

Jhonart shook his head. "Lithann," he said. "You are out of position. Aren't you supposed to patrol the southeastern edge of the forest this cycle?"

"Kennan and I traded," said Lithann. She drew one hand through her hair, her long fingers shifting the long strands back behind both pointed ears.

Jhonart did not have the patience for this today. Lithann was a lovely girl, but she lacked discipline. "Well I suggest you return to your patrol zone, and perhaps practice your stealth along the way. It was far too easy for Artemis to spot your movements."

Jhonart reached into a small pocket in his jerkin, really no more than a fold in the leather, and pulled out a bit of jerky. He reached up and allowed Artemis to snap it out of his grip, the falcon's beak closing just shy of his fingertips.

"Or did I allow Artemis to spy me?" asked Lithann, her eyes twinkling in the shafts of flickering light that had forced their way through the foliage. "Have you not asked yourself where Wiley might be?"

Lithann laughed as her pet fox sprang out from a bush behind Jhonart. The black-striped fox nipped at Jhonart's thick thigh as she caromed off his leg.

Startled by the sudden impact and the sting of teeth, Jhonart nearly lost his balance as he twisted to the side. Artemis, his perch suddenly unstable, flew up into the air in a flurry of wings that buffeted Jhonart in the side of the head, flustering the large elf even more.

"You see, Jhonart?" said Lithann, "Stealth is not the only battle tactic. Misdirection and surprise can be just as effective."

"Enough!" bellowed Jhonart. The force of his voice startled a flock of sparrows into sudden flight in the trees above. "Neither of us is doing our job while we sit here jabbering at one another. Return to your post and let me return to mine."

Lithann's smile disappeared as she lowered her eyes and head to stare at the ground. Wiley, her Bitterwood fox pet, slinked around at her feet, peeking at Jhonart from behind one leg and then another, as if trying to hide but still wanting to be a part of it all.

"I just wanted to say hello," said Lithann. "This cycle has been boring and quiet. I've had nothing to occupy my time and mind other than counting the wind and measuring the sunshine."

Jhonart decided to ignore Lithann's usual nonsensical ramblings. "That is the life of a Beastmaster," he said, the tone of his voice softening a touch. "You know that. Our time out here in the quiet of the forest is a blessing few elves ever get to enjoy. Perhaps if it weighs on you so, then your temperament may be better suited to other pursuits."

Lithann reached over her shoulder to adjust the bow on her back. "I love the forest," she said. "It is the one place I feel at home. It constantly changes in a million small ways, yet ever stays the same. Normally, it fascinates me, but lately, other matters have…"

She trailed off and her eyes, which had risen to look at Jhonart while she talked, fell back to gaze at the ground once more.

"I just wanted to say hello," she said again. "I'm sorry to have bothered you." She turned and began walking away toward the edge of the small clearing. "I shall return to my post now. Perhaps we will see one another during the next arena day."

"I would like that," said Jhonart as Lithann slipped into the trees. He wasn't sure she had heard him, though, as she did not stop.

Jhonart glanced up into the trees to look for Artemis, but the falcon had already left the confines of the forest and begun soaring over the border between the Straywood and the Anvil Throne.

"Back to work," said Jhonart to himself, and then sighed. He never talked to himself on patrol. He shook his head and began working his way back to the edge of the forest, making no sound and leaving no trace of his passing.

Before he reached the tree line, Jhonart heard Artemis screech again. "I have no time for this, Lithann," he muttered, but when Artemis screeched again, the sound was cut off, ending in what sounded like a gurgle.

He began running for the forest's edge, taking no care to hide his passing. He burst from the trees into an expanse of bare ground, low scrub brush, and boulders that gently sloped up toward the towering mountains of the Anvil Throne.

At first, Jhonart saw nothing beyond the glare of the sun reflecting brightly against the flat, featureless ground and the jagged edges of the rocks. He shielded his eyes to help them adjust faster and scanned the area for Artemis. He knew his pet still lived. The bond had not yet been broken. But where was he?

Jhonart moved forward cautiously, his staff held in both hands in front of his body. He considered summoning a feral bobcat to help him search the rocky terrain, but decided to conserve his mana for the moment.

Instead, the elf Beastmaster closed his eyes and concentrated on his pet senses. When he opened his eyes again, Jhonart was looking up into the grotesque face of a monster through the eyes of his pet.

It looked almost dwarflike, but had bat ears and a pair of mandibles extending from its mouth. Instead of fingers and hands, long, sharp claws extended from its paws, which were wrapped around Artemis, holding the falcon firmly around his wings and neck. Behind the monster, Jhonart could see many more of the abominations to nature hiding behind the very same sun-drenched rocks and boulders he had been shielding his eyes against a moment before.

Realizing his mistake, Jhonart broke the connection as quickly as he could, but it was too late. The creatures swarmed over and around the rocks, seemingly coming from everywhere at once. Their claws allowed them to climb as fast as they could run, and they somehow coordinated their movements to cut off any retreat without even speaking. In a moment, Jhonart was surrounded.

As the creatures began to close on Jhonart, he quickly conjured a wall of thorns to slow down the attackers on his left. He then turned to his right, advanced on the flanking creatures and struck one of them across the mandibles with his staff. Surprisingly, the creature fell to the ground unconscious. Perhaps he might actually live through this.

The monsters to either side and behind the unconscious creature paid no attention to their downed comrade. They simply stepped over its body and attacked.

Claws ripped at Jhonart's body, but his bearskin jerkin turned most of their attacks aside. One managed to poke right through the armor, though, and gouge out a large chunk of flesh just under his ribs.

Jhonart conjured vines to entangle one of the creatures in front of him, and then began an incantation. He needed to create a hole in the monsters' line so he could escape. He had only one chance to get this right. Unfortunately, as he started the spell, the other two monsters in front of him moved to attack.

The attacks never landed, though. Artemis had managed to escape and dove into the face of Jhonart's attacker at that very moment. The falcon's beak tore at the creature's face, ripping off a mandible before spearing the beast right through the bat ears and into its brain. The monster fell in a heap.

The other creature turned away from Jhonart and raked its claws through the air, impaling poor Artemis through the chest and neck before the falcon had a chance to fly up out of reach. Jhonart's pet fell to the ground at his feet just as the elf finished his incantation.

A moment later, all of the monsters in front of Jhonart fell to the ground, asleep. However, the long incantation had given the monsters behind him a chance to get closer. A half-dozen of them tore and clawed and ripped at his armor and flesh, scoring multiple deep wounds.

Bloody and sore all over, Jhonart took a single moment to cast rhino hide on himself to harden his skin before running, full-tilt, through the field of sleeping creatures and away from his attackers. The monsters behind the elf gave chase, but once Jhonart got enough distance on them, he took a moment to conjure another wall of thorns between himself and his pursuers.

Clear of the trap and with a little time to breathe before the monsters fought through the thorny barrier, Jhonart stopped to summon a beast to fight for him. A moment later, a huge, brown bear stood before Jhonart. Unfortunately, he had underestimated the speed of his attackers once again and saw them flanking him and cutting off his path back toward the forest.

Jhonart cast a quick incantation to rouse his bear companion from the disorientation caused by its summoning and commanded it to guard its position.

The first monster to arrive attacked the bear and was literally torn apart by the grizzly's claws, its arms and legs flying into the air and raining down on the other attackers. A few ignored the falling flesh and attacked Jhonart, but their attacks could not penetrate both his armor and his enhanced hide.

The rest of the monsters moved to flank the elf once again, but the bear made that more difficult, giving Jhonart an opening to escape once again.

As he ran, Jhonart scanned the battlefield, looking for a path that would take him both away from his pursuers and back toward the safety of the forest. However, the monsters had done a magnificent job of closing down all avenues of escape, except the northeasterly path that led farther up into the foothills.

Just as Jhonart realized that the creatures had been herding him onto that path all along, he rounded a boulder and discovered why.

Before he could stop himself, Jhonart ran headlong over the edge of a gaping four-meter diameter hole in the ground behind the boulder. As he plunged into the pit, Jhonart had time for a single thought: How deep must a hole be for the bottom to be enveloped in pitch-blackness at noon on a cloudless day? Then, everything went dark.

CHAPTER 2: DESCENT INTO DARKNESS

Lithann strode through the forest, paying little attention to her surroundings or her path. Wiley padded beside her, periodically nudging her legs to keep the distracted wood elf from running into briers, tripping over fallen limbs, or stumbling into burrow holes.

"I thought he was different, Wiley," she said as she walked. Hearing her name, the fox looked up, her open, panting mouth looking every bit like a smile. Lithann ruffled her pet's ears.

"Jhonart and I had such a wonderful discussion at the last arena day. He actually answered my questions instead of ignoring me or pushing me toward someone else who 'would better know the answer to that,' and then quickly disappearing back into the crowd."

Wiley stopped suddenly in front of Lithann, her bushy, red-and-black striped tail standing straight up. Lithann bumped into the rear of her pet before stopping.

"What?" she asked before looking. "Oh. Thank you, Wiley." She flipped a stray strand of her long, black hair back over her ear again before jumping over the small stream at her feet. Wiley followed a moment later.

The two of them walked in silence for a few moments before Lithann began again, her anger fuming just behind her eyes. "I swear, everyone in this forest has told me at one time or another that I lack patience. But ask a few pointed questions like, 'Instead of patrolling our borders, why don't we simply make peace with our neighbors?' or 'If the Darkfenne is such a problem, why don't we ask for help?' or 'Where is it written that Beastmasters must patrol alone? Wouldn't it make more sense to patrol in pairs?' and people lose patience with you pretty quickly. Sometimes I swear my father pushed me into border patrol just so I would stop embarrassing him in front of the rest of wood elf society."

Lithann stopped and took a deep breath to clear her head and then looked down at her fox friend. Wiley sat and smile-panted up at Lithann. She scratched the fox behind one ear. "I'm glad you never tire of hearing me talk, Wiley," she said. "Otherwise, I might go crazy out here alone."

In the distance, a falcon screeched. Lithann and Wiley turned their heads at the sound. When they heard the half-screech that followed a moment later, they glanced at each other before running back the way they had come.

As they retraced their path, Lithann became painfully aware of every briar, burrow hole, and broken limb that Wiley had guided her around during their earlier, leisurely hike. Now they became more than mere annoyances—they stymied her progress, making her feel as if they were crawling through the forest.

She began to hear sounds of a battle coming not from the forest ahead of her, but from the open expanse of the Anvil Throne lowlands to the east.

Lithann changed direction and began heading toward the forest's edge. At least out in the open, she could make better time back to where she had left Jhonart and Artemis.

A moment later, Lithann and Wiley broke out of the forest into the open, rock-strewn expanse beyond the tree line. She skidded to a stop after only a few steps. While Lithann had gazed out of the forest from nearly all along the border, she had never actually stepped foot outside the safe confines of the Straywood.

She felt almost naked without the trees and underbrush surrounding her, enveloping her, cloaking her. Everything was so bright that Lithann could hardly discern rocks from ground, boulders from sky. She glanced up at the sun, seeing it for the first time without its light being filtered through layer upon layer of leaves and vines and branches. She closed her eyes quickly as yellow blotches formed in the middle of her vision.

She blinked away the blotches and fought to calm her mind. If being alone made Lithann stir-crazy, then being caught out in the open with no trees to protect her and nothing above her but clouds and sky, terrified her. Although she had to admit that her heart was racing not just from fear, but from excitement as well.

As Lithann's vision cleared and adjusted to the sudden brightness outside the forest, she could finally make out the battle to the north of her.

Several dozen small, misshapen creatures scampered about and scrabbled over and around the rocks. A handful of the nasty creatures fought a giant grizzly bear off to one side. She recognized the bear. It was one of Jhonart's favorite creatures to summon.

So, where was Jhonart? It shouldn't be that hard to find one tall, broad-shouldered, square-jawed elf amongst all those small, hunched-over creatures.

Then, she saw him, running away from the horde. Even from this distance, she could see blood flowing freely from numerous tears in his armor and cuts in his arms. He was too far away to heal or help, so Lithann began running again.

Before she'd taken three strides, though, she watched Jhonart round a boulder. She saw the gaping hole in the ground before he did. She tried to cry out, but the heat from the sun coupled with her recent mad dash through the forest had dried out her throat. All she could manage was a dry rasping sound.

Then Jhonart tumbled over the edge of the chasm and dropped out of sight. Lithann redoubled her speed, but as soon as Jhonart fell, all the foul creatures ran to the hole and climbed over the edge. They didn't fall. They didn't stop and lower themselves down. They simply ran on all fours to the edge of the hole and then straight down into it, without ever slowing down.

A moment later the grizzly and the thorny walls vanished. Everything Jhonart had summoned during the battle returned back to the ether from whence mages summon them. Jhonart was either dead or unconscious. It was the only explanation.

Lithann arrived at the scene of the battle a few seconds after Jhonart fell, but found nothing left—no sign of the huge fight—save one dead bird.

Wiley knelt and sniffed at the corpse of Artemis, and then sat down and howled. "Shush," said Lithann. "Guard him from scavengers while I check out that hole."

Wiley began prowling around the bird, watching both the sky and the ground, possibly unsure where a scavenger attack might come from, and completely oblivious to the fact that any other fox would already be ripping meat off the bird's bones.

Lithann loped quietly across the hard ground toward the huge hole. As she got close, she dropped to her hands and knees and crawled to the edge. Peering over, she could see only six to nine meters down into the hole. The sun illuminated most of one side, showing rough-hewn rock and dirt walls that looked like they had literally been clawed into existence. Sets of long grooves overlapped and intersected up and down the entire length of the chasm walls.

Fortunately, Lithann didn't see any of the foul creatures that had chased Jhonart down into the hole. Unfortunately, the hole continued down past where the light from the sun could penetrate, so she couldn't see either Jhonart or his pursuers, although she swore she heard scrabbling sounds echoing back up the hole.

Lithann knew she should report this at once, but if she took the time to return to an outpost, she would have no chance of ever catching up to the beasts and finding Jhonart.

She had an idea, though.

Lithann returned to the dead falcon and began an incantation. She wasn't sure it would work because she'd never used it on another Beastmaster's pet. But she had to try.

The sun beat down on Lithann's raven-hair-covered head as she cast the spell. The heat of the sun and her intense concentration caused several beads of sweat to form on her forehead and trail down past her eyes and over her cheeks. She finished the spell, wiped her brow, and waited.

A moment later, Artemis's wingtips folded ever so slightly and then straightened out. Then his tail flapped violently. Lithann watched as the falcon's wounds closed up and he turned his head to push at the ground with his beak. She reached down and helped the bird turn over onto his feet and Artemis screed in response.

Lithann decided that was his way of saying thank you. Then the large, white and gold bird jumped into the air and flapped his wings. Artemis turned his head back and forth, as if looking for something, or someone.

"Artemis!" commanded Lithann. "Wait!"

The bird landed at her feet and looked up at her.

"Jhonart has been captured," she guessed or lied, not willing to tell the Beastmaster's pet her worst fears. "I need you to take a message back to the nearest outpost. I am going to go after Jhonart and bring him home."

Artemis bobbed his head in response. Lithann pulled out some parchment and a quill from her pack and began scribbling a quick note.

*　　*　　*　　*　　*　　*

After attaching the note to Artemis's leg and watching the falcon fly back into the forest, Lithann and Wiley walked back to the hole. "Now," she said to herself as much as Wiley, "how do we get down to the bottom of this hole?"

Lithann thought she might be able to climb down. She climbed trees often enough. But it wasn't like there were any branches or knotholes to hold onto. The gouges in the side walls of the chasm all ran vertically, providing no real purchase for small, elf hands. And no matter what, she wouldn't be able to carry Wiley down with her.

Then a thought occurred to her. Perhaps she needed something that could carry *her* down to the bottom, both her and her pet fox. She smiled at Wiley. "I have an idea, but I'm afraid you might not like it," she said. "I need you to trust me."

Wiley panted at her and pawed the ground at the edge of the hole. Lithann took that as a "get on with it already," and began casting a summoning spell.

A moment later, a giant mountain gorilla appeared next to the two of them. It beat its bare chest with huge, clawed paws, making the thick, brown fur covering its arms flow back and forth like waves crashing on the shores of the Diamond Sea.

Just to make sure the gorilla could carry both of them, Lithann gave it the strength of a bear before commanding it to pick her up. The gorilla reached down with one giant paw and grabbed the elf around the waist. It hoisted her up over its furry shoulder and then used the same paw to grab her fox by the scruff of the neck. Wiley yelped in protest, but a gentle word from Lithann quieted her pet.

Before Lithann could change her mind, the gorilla turned and stepped over the edge of the chasm backward, catching the lip of the hole with its other massive paw, its claws digging into the dirt and rock.

Lithann closed her eyes on the way down, partly because the view of the seemingly bottomless pit lurching back and forth beneath the back of the gorilla was making her ill, and partly to get her eyes adjusted to the dark before they reached the bottom.

After what seemed like an eternity, but was in reality probably only a minute, the gorilla reached the bottom. Lithann heard Wiley yelp a little again and then felt the gorilla lift her off its shoulder. She opened her eyes and could just make out the outline of the rock wall meeting a mostly level patch of ground beneath her feet as the gorilla sat her down.

Before her eyes could adjust any further, Lithann heard a scrabbling sound coming from behind her. She turned to see several dark shapes moving quickly against the blackness. She didn't hesitate a moment, calling out to her two companions, "Attack!"

Wiley shot down the tunnel and ripped into the first shape, snapping at the shadowy creature as it scrambled on all fours toward the hole. Lithann heard the unmistakable sound of a neck snapping. Two other creatures emerged from the tunnel, allowing Lithann her first good look at them, as enough light filtered down to the bottom of the hole to see more than just shapes.

They were misshapen, chimerical creatures that seemed to be molded like clay out of numerous creatures, including ant mandibles, badger claws, and the large, black eyes of owls. Lithann was repulsed by these abominations of nature, but could only think of Jhonart at their mercy.

The gorilla pounded both fists down on top of the first creature before it could attack, splitting its skull and cracking its spine. It dropped to the ground; a bloody, pulpy mass beneath the gorilla's huge paws.

The second advanced on Lithann and swiped at her with its digging claws. The force of the blow surprised the elf—it knocked the wind from her and ripped through her armor into her side.

Lithann regained her composure. Quicker than the creature could react, she pulled her bow over her head, nocked an arrow and sighted down its shaft. The elf pulled the bowstring back with an ease belied by her lithe form and let it loose.

The fletching on the arrow barely cleared the bow before embedding in the forehead of the grotesque creature in front of Lithann. The undiminished force of the pull sent the arrow clean through its skull, and the arrowhead emerged out the back of its neck with a spray of blood and brains.

Lithann glanced around the shadowy gloom, but didn't see any more attackers. She quieted her heart and listened for the telltale scrabbling of the hunched monsters. Hearing nothing, she cast a minor healing spell on herself and checked her two animal companions for wounds.

Once satisfied with their general health, Lithann peered into the darkness and thought about her next move. She needed to track the creatures, which she could do in the forest, even in dim light. But down here in the pitch black, with no bent foliage or impressions in the dirt to follow, she didn't know where to even begin.

Wiley looped around Lithann's legs, her tail wrapping around the elf's calves as she paced. Lithann idly reached her hand down to scratch Wiley's ears as she thought. Then, a smile spread across her face and she leaned down, grabbed her pet by the head and kissed her on the nose.

"You ran off right away when the attack came, didn't you?" The fox smiled her panting smile up at Lithann. "You can see down here, at least better than I can, you sly, nocturnal beast, can't you?"

Wiley's eye sparkled in the dim light. "And I bet you can track these foul creatures. They sure smell bad enough."

"All right, Wiley," said Lithann, pointing at the dead monster at her feet. "Get a good sniff. We're going hunting!"

CHAPTER 3: LET THERE BE LIGHT

Lithann felt her way along behind the fox. She could hear Wiley's claws against the bare rock floor as she padded her way down the subterranean tunnel, but the elf could only stumble along behind in the total darkness. She had to run her hand along the smooth walls and tap at the bare, flat stone floor with her toes before every step. They weren't so much chasing Jhonart's captors as crawling after them.

It wasn't just dim here, like on a moonless night when the stars provided tiny pinpricks of light across the sky, enough to allow the eye to discern shadows and shapes. Even a cloudy night wasn't completely dark. The clouds gathered and held light from every campfire, lamp, and candle in the forest, giving the sky a comfortable pale gray glow over villages and outposts that could be seen for miles.

Here, though, there was no light, no lamps, nothing but darkness closing in around her.

To add to her troubles, Wiley kept straying off. Perhaps the fox became frustrated with their slow pace or perhaps she just felt the need to scout ahead for danger while her master lagged behind, hobbled by blindness. Whatever the reason, every time Lithann realized she could no longer hear her pet's clicking claws and panting breath, she had to stop and call Wiley back to her side before they could begin their slow, trudging hike again.

After a while, even the gorilla became agitated with their start-and-stop pace and the general lack of creatures to attack. It began huffing every few seconds to show impatience, and started beating on its chest when the huffing failed to speed things up. Shortly after the gorilla halted and let out a huge roar, Lithann dismissed the beast.

In the sudden silence that followed, Lithann realized that Wiley had disappeared again. She called to her pet: "Wiley! Come!"

Nothing happened. How far ahead had the fox gotten? "Wiley, return!" she called again. "Wiley!" Her voice echoed in the darkness, but she heard no answer, nor the sound of claws clicking their way back toward her, as she had several times before.

"Great!" she said to herself. "Now I have no light and no guide." Lithann knew she could simply re-summon her pet, but that wouldn't alleviate the bigger issue. Without light, she would never find Jhonart, let alone fight an army of misshapen beasts.

Then Lithann remembered she had brought a light source with her. It had been hanging around her neck all this time. She uttered a simple command word and the tunnel brightened slightly around her. She lowered her chin to look down at the smooth leather stretched across her lithe frame. There, underneath her armor, a dim glow emanated from her chest.

"How could I have forgotten about you?" she asked out loud. She pulled on the chain around her neck, raising the glow up toward her chin. Silver filigree wings caught for a moment on the collar of her armor before popping free, allowing the glowing pearl nestled among the wings to light up the tunnel around her. She rarely needed the light of the moonglow amulet, but today this secondary ability of her mana stone turned out to be a blessing.

Lithann glanced around at her surroundings. The walls on either side of her ran straight and true. At the edge of her light, Lithann could see milled wooden timbers strapped to both side walls with iron bands. These straight-cut logs supported a huge beam that spanned the ceiling of the tunnel.

Glancing behind, she found another set of supports near at hand and a third at the edge of her light. Lithann had felt the wood periodically as she ran her hands along the wall earlier, but had no idea what they were for, and her slow pace had made it impossible to tell how close together they had been placed.

This tunnel looked nothing like the grooved sides of the chasm. These straight, smooth walls, with their precise angles and machined support timbers had been methodically constructed over time with advanced tools, not hastily dug by bare claws.

It began to dawn on Lithann that while she had been tracking some sort of unknown feral beasts, she had been actually walking through tunnels cut by the residents of the Anvil Throne. She was trespassing in dwarven lands, alone. If she were caught, death would be the least of her concerns. Her actions, however altruistic, could start a war between the dwarves and the elves.

Everything inside Lithann told her to run back the way she had come, climb back out of the hole, and race back to the outpost. But that would certainly doom Jhonart to death at the hands of those horrible creatures. Plus, what more could she tell the elders other than what she'd written in the note? What were those creatures? Were they dwarven pets or some sort of beast army the dwarves had raised to expand their territory? Was Jhonart's abduction a prelude to war?

Lithann knew she couldn't leave. Not yet. Perhaps another elf would have turned back. If Jhonart were here, he would definitely have counseled caution. But Lithann could never turn away from unanswered questions. However, she couldn't move forward without Wiley to help her track the beasts, so she tried calling again.

"Wiley!" she yelled. "Come here, girl."

Nothing. After her echoing cry faded away, the dank air in the tunnel became still and silent once more. Just as she was about to re-summon her pet, Lithann heard a scrabbling noise echoing down the tunnel. Faint at first, it grew louder and louder.

Lithann peered down the tunnel, trying to see past the edge of her light, hopeful that the clicking of claws on stone signaled the return of her lost fox and not the foul creatures that had taken Jhonart. The noise grew louder and still Lithann saw no sign of fox or monster. Then, when the echoing sound was almost on top of her, Lithann realized it was coming from behind!

She twisted around, pulling her bow out as she turned, just as the slim, red-and-black striped body of her pet padded into the light.

"Where have you been?" asked Lithann as she scratched Wiley's ears. The fox just panted at her, and then turned around, and began walking back the way she had come. "No!" said Lithann. "We're not going back. I've already decided. Come on. I can see now. I'll lead the way."

Lithann turned and headed down the tunnel, the renewed vigor of determination entering her step. After a moment, the fox turned and followed, falling into step at her heels.

*   *   *   *   *   *

After walking for what seemed like an hour or more, Lithann and Wiley came to an intersection in the tunnel. Although Lithann had trouble telling time down here, cut off from the movement of the sun and stars, so it could have been several hours or even a fraction of an hour; time had no meaning in the dark.

Two other tunnels opened up at odd angles on either side of Lithann, while the tunnel she had been walking along for the last hour or more continued on as straight and true as ever into the darkness. Lithann stopped and listened, hoping to hear something—anything—to help her make a decision on which way to go. She heard nothing coming from any of the tunnels.

Lithann had been quite good at solving the hedge mazes during summer festivals as a child, but those contained far more clues than these tunnels. She could tell north from east for one thing, and the scents of surrounding vegetation often provided clues as to which way to turn.

Down here, though, direction was difficult to detect, and the only thing she could smell was the musky odor of never-quite-dry cloth and wood with just a hint of dung. At first, the odor had almost been too much for her and she had gagged several times in the first hour. But now, it had faded to a background stench that she only noticed when breathing deeply through her nose.

Hearing nothing, Lithann stepped into each of the intersecting tunnels one at a time to take a deep breath. The tunnel to her left ran straight and level, but it turned back at such a sharp angle that the wall came to almost a razor-fine point where it met the other tunnel. She wasn't sure backtracking was the best idea. Plus, the air in this tunnel smelled no differently than the one she had been trudging through for hours, so Lithann decided to check the other two.

The tunnel running straight ahead seemed to have a slight incline. She wondered if it would eventually take her back to the surface, but one sniff told Lithann it would most definitely never return to the surface. If anything, the moldy, dung-heavy scent was much stronger in this tunnel. Plus, she detected a combination of additional odors emanating from not too far ahead that made her pause. This tunnel smelled of charred meat and burning oil—two strong indications of intelligent creatures, which meant dwarves. She did not want to go that way.

That just left the tunnel to the right, which formed an almost perpendicular intersection to the middle tunnel. However, it had a definite downgrade, which would take her deeper underground. She took a deep breath to see if the air provided any other clues, but the air coming up this tunnel was nearly indistinguishable to the tunnel leading back to the left. There might have been a hint of something—wax maybe? She wasn't sure.

Lithann was about to go back to the first tunnel, thinking that heading away from the dwarves was the best plan, at least as a first choice. Then she saw something glittering in the darkness down the right path. It was only there for a moment and then it was gone. Perhaps she just imagined it, but then she saw it again.

"What is that?" she asked, but no one answered. Even Wiley seemed disinterested. He padded back to the original tunnel and sat down facing back the way they had come. "I know what you want," said Lithann. She turned back to watch for the light to appear again, but could see nothing.

On a hunch, Lithann commanded her moonglow amulet to darken. In the pitch black, she could now see something in the distance. It was some sort of light, flickering like a dying fire or a torch far off in the distance. It seemed worth investigating anyway and, Lithann figured, if it were dwarves, the light would be stronger, steadier, and brighter.

She called softly to Wiley and began down the path to her right. She walked in the dark, not wanting to warn anyone or anything of her approach by lighting her amulet again. It would be slow going, but the flickering fire provided enough light to keep her from stumbling about, even at this distance.

*   *   *   *   *   *

After walking a while, the flickering light in the distance began to get larger, but moved to the side. Lithann wondered if the tunnel turned ahead, but as she got closer, she realized the truth: The light was coming from a chamber off the main tunnel. In fact, that chamber was so bright that light from inside spilled out into the tunnel and could be seen from a long way off.

Lithann crept up to the glowing doorway and peered inside. The chamber was an absolute treasure trove filled with gold candelabras, gem-encrusted goblets, and ivory statues. The walls of the cavern were draped in silk tapestries that depicted battle scenes and festivals. The light came from dozens upon dozens of burning candles set in the various candelabras around the room.

An ornately carved, obsidian table stood in the middle of the chamber. Symbols etched in bas-relief, ran down the side of each leg, and another set of symbols ran across the edge of the tabletop. Lithann had no idea what the symbols meant, if anything.

Two huge candelabras flanked the table, each holding a dozen burning candles in an intricate, diamond-shaped array. The top candles towered over the table, their holders standing a full two and a half meters above the ground.

The table held twelve golden goblets all with the same intricate diamond-shaped design shown in the candelabra. A large golden statue of a dwarf in flowing robes stood behind the table. The statue held a hammer aloft in one hand, while clutching a tome or tablet against its side in the other.

Seeing no living dwarves in the chamber, Lithann slipped inside to get a better look at the table and the tapestries. Perhaps somewhere in here she would find a clue to the whereabouts of the monstrous creatures that had taken Jhonart, or at least the connection between the creatures and the dwarves.

She moved along the wall, studying each tapestry in turn. She hoped to find an image of one of the creatures in the battle scenes to see if they were fighting beside or against the dwarves. But all the battles were between dwarves and orcs. She saw goblins on both sides, along with a myriad of other creatures, such as minotaurs, earth elementals, and golems. But no sign of the chimera-like creatures with bat ears, ant mandibles, and badger claws.

Lithann stopped in front of the obsidian table, which she figured must be an altar, and looked at the goblets. What she failed to see from the doorway was that they were also arrayed in the same diamond pattern.

Just as she reached out to pick up the nearest goblet, Lithann heard what sounded like a gasp behind her.

"Don't touch that!" said a gravelly voice.

Lithann whirled around to see a male dwarf standing in the doorway illuminated by the hundreds of candles in the chamber. He wore a flowing, hooded robe over a black leather jerkin and breeches. Lithann could see the horror in the dwarf's wide eyes and gaping mouth, even though his face was shadowed by the hood.

If that horror was from the presence of an elf in his temple chamber or the fact that she had almost touched one of his sacred relics, Lithann wasn't sure. In fact, she was only assuming this was a temple and he some sort of priest or monk. Perhaps all dwarves wore flowing, hooded robes. This was the first one she had ever met.

Lithann looked at the dwarf and the doorway and tried to determine whether she could simply bolt through and disappear in the darkness. But of course, that was ridiculous, as the dwarf would most assuredly be able to see much better in the dark than she could.

Wiley must have sensed her master's trepidation because she began to creep forward, her tail held low as she took slow, halting steps. The dwarf turned toward the fox stalking him like a prey and pulled a double-edged blade from beneath his cloak. At a word, it began to glow. He held the weapon in one hand in front of him, the blades curving away in opposite directions.

Lithann hoped to defuse the situation before it got out of control. She did not want to be the elf responsible for rekindling the war between the two races.

"I mean you no harm," she said. "I am merely searching for a friend of mine who was abducted by some foul creatures that clawed their way out of the ground at the edge of the forest."

At the mention of the chimeras, the dwarf cocked his head and Lithann noticed his hand drop down a bit, lowering his blade slightly.

Lithann called out to Wiley. "Stay!" she commanded. "Sit!"

The fox glanced over her shoulder as if to ask, "Are you sure? He looks like an enemy."

Lithann nodded at her pet and motioned for her to heel. Reluctantly, Wiley turned around and padded back to her side.

"I am going to remove my weapon," said Lithann to the dwarf. "I simply want information. I think you know something about the creatures who took my friend."

The dwarf nodded, but did not douse his weapon or stow it away.

Lithann understood. Trust had to be earned. She reached over her shoulder and grabbed her bow in one hand. She lifted it high up over her head and then dramatically tossed it to the side. She smiled and placed both hands, palm forward in front of her to show she had no weapons.

The gesture did not have the desired effect on the dwarf, however. Instead, he gasped again and bolted into the chamber, his two-headed blade flipping up and down in the air as he ran.

At first, Lithann thought he was attacking, but the dwarf ran toward the back corner of the chamber. Lithann turned, wondering if he was trying an elaborate feint. But then she saw what had happened.

Her bow had knocked several candles off the large candelabra to her left, which ignited one of the tapestries. Flames and smoke threatened to engulf the room.

CHAPTER 4: TRIAL BY FIRE

Living in the forest, Lithann knew all too well the dangers of fire. One unquenched spark could destroy hundreds if not thousands of hectares. Elves minded their fires closely and never left anything burning unattended.

It wasn't just their lives and homes the elves worried about during a fire. They depended on the forest for everything, and everything in the forest lived in a natural balance with every other thing.

Fire destroyed that equilibrium. It affected every creature and every plant, burning their homes, destroying their food supply, and fouling their habitats for months if not years to come.

So, as she saw the fire, Lithann knew exactly what to do. She had trained for this her entire life. It was the one lesson taught to every wood elf from the first day of training.

Unfortunately, before Lithann could do anything to stop the dwarf, he had already reached the tapestry, grabbed it by a non-burning corner, and ripped it off the wall.

Lithann assumed the dwarf hoped to wrap it up and smother the fire. Unfortunately, when he pulled it down, the burning tapestry fell on top of the candelabra, igniting the rest of the fabric and knocking the now incredibly top-heavy and flaming candelabra to the floor.

Wiley yelped and fled into the tunnel as flaming shreds of tapestry flew across the room and burning candles rolled into every corner of the chamber. Within seconds, a half-dozen other tapestries had caught fire and the room began to fill with smoke and flames.

If the destruction of a fragile eco-system was the main danger of fire in the forest, Lithann learned quickly today that smoke was the thing to fear when fire erupted underground in enclosed spaces.

Before she could even react, Lithann began choking on the black fumes that billowed up and collected on the ceiling from at least six different fires throughout the small chamber. A large black cloud hung above them and Lithann could see it growing ever larger and closer as its volume increased.

Lithann knew she had to act fast before the fire got even more out of control. She dropped to her hands and knees to get some space between her and the billowing cloud of black smoke, crawled to the middle of the room, and began focusing her mind to gather magical energy.

Tendrils of mana flowed from her fingertips and enveloped her hands in a glowing aura. She braced herself for the coming impact and uttered the words to cast the spell.

An instant later, a torrent of water erupted underneath Lithann. The column of water hit the ceiling and spread across the room, turning the cloud of smoke to steam before raining down around her and dousing the flames.

The various fires hissed as the geyser rain fell on the tapestries, soaking the fabric and extinguishing the flames. Within moments, the fires were all out, and the smoke had all cleared. The only remnants of the fire were soaked pieces of scorched tapestry floating in a soggy mess of black water that coated the floor.

After making sure that none of the fires still burned, Lithann glanced around to check on the dwarf and look for Wiley. She saw the dwarf in the back of chamber, his head bowed as he surveyed the wreckage. Lithann walked over to him, patted him on the back, and said, "I'm sorry. Here. Let me help."

She grabbed the top of the candelabra and, with the help of the dwarven monk stood it back up next to the altar. Lithann grabbed her bow as the dwarf began picking up candles and pushing tapestry remnants into the corners. After securing her bow on her back, Lithann took a couple of candles the dwarf had placed on the altar. As she began setting them back in their holders, Lithann heard footsteps entering the room behind her.

She turned to see a stern-looking female dwarf dressed in fine, supple leathers and wearing a golden amulet around her neck. The ornate nature and obvious weight of the amulet made it appear to be more ceremonial than magical. She was flanked by four male dwarves in battle armor who were wielding spears.

The female spoke in short, clipped tones. "Take the elf into custody for crimes against the Anvil Throne!"

The four guards surrounded Lithann and one of them produced a pair of manacles. Lithann extended her arms and let herself be shackled. She had no choice. Resisting would do nothing but escalate the situation. Wars had been started over less. It seemed best to simply cooperate.

The dwarven monk didn't see it that way. "This is my fault," he exclaimed as he ran over to the female dwarf, dropping a load of candles in his haste to intervene. "She saved my life when the fire spread throughout the temple!"

The female, who Lithann assumed to be some sort of magistrate, held her hand up in front of the monk's face. "Be that as it may," she said, cutting off any more interruptions, "she is a trespasser in our lands and must stand trial for her crimes."

The monk was about to say something more, when the magistrate shouted, "Silence! I have ruled. If you have any decency left inside you, Digur, you will abide by my rulings and keep your opinions to yourself!"

She motioned to the guards to follow and left the chamber. Two of the guards grabbed Lithann by the arms and marched her out of while the other two fell in step behind them. The monk sputtered a few times, but apparently was so cowed by the magistrate that he couldn't form any more words.

As they left the chamber, Lithann glanced up the tunnel she had walked down earlier and saw two vulpine eyes glowing in the dark. She motioned with her eyes as best she could for Wiley to follow. She knew the fox could remain out of sight and outrun anything down here if she did get spotted. She would be fine.

*   *   *   *   *   *

The magistrate led the guards down the tunnel into the darkness. Lithann didn't dare light her amulet for fear that the guards might take it away from her. In fact, she had subtly tucked it back under her armor before they manacled her.

So, after they moved away from the temple, she couldn't really see at all and stumbled quite often in the dark, especially at the brisk pace the magistrate had set. Luckily the guards kept Lithann on her feet each time they tangled beneath her. The dwarven guards were shorter than Lithann, but even holding her arms up high for them, they had remarkable strength.

After a while, they turned left, and Lithann could feel air moving in other directions when they yanked her off to the side, so she was certain they had passed another intersection.

A few minutes later, they turned sharply to the right. Lithann could see some lights flickering in the distance in at least four other directions at that intersection. She tried to keep each turn in mind, so she could find her way back out again should she find some way to escape dwarven justice.

After the second turn, they began passing more side chambers, some small like the temple and some cavernous. Most of these were at least partially lit along the walls, so Lithann could finally see a bit again.

The tunnel itself had gotten much larger. She couldn't even see the ceiling above her in the darker areas, but when they passed a lit chamber, she could see it was easily six meters tall.

After several more turns in quick succession, Lithann was quite lost, but the magistrate finally slowed down. She stopped just past the entrance to another cavern. Lithann could see torches high up in the distance through the doorway. This was a huge chamber.

"Take her into the arena," said the magistrate before turning on her heels and marching off.

The guards pulled Lithann through the doorway into the cavernous chamber. As advertised, it was an arena—a gigantic, open, square space big enough to summon monsters and walls and even structures within. It was easily a hundred meters square and forty meters high, carved completely out of rock.

Torches hung high up on the walls at regular intervals around the arena. Above the torch level, the walls opened up to reveal large sections of seating nestled between support columns.

As Lithann was guided to the middle of the arena floor, she noticed a group of dwarves seated in the middle section along the back wall. As she watched, the magistrate entered the seating area from above the group and climbed down the steps to sit in the middle.

She lifted a large rock off a low stone table set in front of the group and banged it back down. A dull thrum echoed around the arena chamber and reverberated through the rocks. Lithann could feel the impact of the rock on the table as much as feel it.

The magistrate lifted the rock again and slammed it back down one more time. Lithann almost felt like the entire mountain resonated with the second strike.

A few moments passed and nothing happened. Then, dwarves began appearing in the back of the seating areas, in ones and twos at first, and then in larger and larger groups. Some milled around at the top of the chamber, while others moved down to take seats.

Most crowded around the windows cut into the arena walls at the very bottom of the seating areas. Lithann realized she must be the first elf most of these dwarves had ever seen. Out of the corner of her eye, Lithann noticed Digur, the dwarf from the temple, slip into the back of one of the chambers.

She wouldn't have been able to tell him apart from any other robed dwarf if not for the scorched sleeves. He had his hood pulled low across his forehead obscuring his face, but when she recognized him, he pulled the hood up a bit and nodded at her.

"I call this trial to order," said the magistrate. "I, Minister Grimhammer, under authority of High King Bellowspark do hereby convene the council of elders to rule upon the acts of war committed in our domain by this elf."

"I committed no acts of war!" protested Lithann. She noticed that she now stood alone in the center of the arena. The guards had retreated to the two doorways on opposite corners of the great chamber.

"Silence!" yelled Grimhammer. "The accused will have her chance to speak at the appropriate time. Councilman Glitterdust, read the charges."

A dour-looking, old dwarf with a long, white beard sitting at the end of the table stood and opened a large tome in front of him. He wore a jet-black cloak trimmed in gray silk or satin, and had no fewer than eight gold rings inlaid with a variety of precious gems on his pudgy fingers. The rings glittered in the flickering light as he flipped through the pages of the tome.

When he got to the right page, councilman Glitterdust stroked his beard a few times and cracked a sly, chilling smile before speaking.

"The accused is charged with illegally crossing the border into the domain of the Anvil Throne without formal writ of passage; criminal trespass in the outer tunnels of the realm with the intent of mischief, destruction of public property in the Temple of Twelve Diamonds, and espionage in the first degree."

Lithann opened her mouth to protest again, but the minister cut her off before she could speak.

"How do you plead?" asked Minister Grimhammer.

"Is it my turn to speak now?" asked Lithann, each word dripping with sarcasm.

"You may enter a plea," replied the minister, calmly.

Lithann knew anger would not help her here, especially in front of a hostile crowd, but she ground her teeth and felt the heat rising on the back of her neck as she stared at the smug face of the minister.

She forced herself to calm down so she could think. She took a couple of slow breaths, trying to feel every last bit of air enter and leave her lungs to help slow down her racing heart.

It was obvious from the charges and the speed of their response in the temple that the dwarves had been aware of her presence in the tunnels all along. They must also be aware of the chimerical creatures that had taken Jhonart. This trial might be a chance to find out if the creatures were connected to the dwarves or not.

Lithann considered her next words carefully before speaking. "I plead extenuating circumstances," she said after a moment, repeating a phrase she had heard once during the trial of a wood elf who had burned a section of the Great Forest to prevent the spread of plant-rotting disease.

Her vague statement had the desired effect on the judges, who all looked at one another. Some shrugged, while others creased their eyebrows questioningly. A couple just sat with their mouths open, while the minister simply glared at her.

From what Lithann had heard about the dwarves, they were slaves to ceremony. Everything had to be done in accordance with the rules. She'd seen it for herself today, and the look on the minister's face told her she had found her opening.

They couldn't move on to the trial without a proper plea, and they now wouldn't get a plea until Lithann had a chance to tell her side of the story.

The minister sighed so loud that Lithann heard it from over fifty meters away. "Explain yourself, elf," she said.

Lithann took another deep breath before beginning. She wanted to get as much of this out as possible before getting cut off.

"Yes, I have entered your realm without permission," she began, "but I am on a mission of mercy. My friend was abducted from the border of our lands by foul creatures that fled into your tunnels."

The minister tried to cut her off, but Lithann pushed on. "These foul creatures have badger claws, ant mandibles, and owl eyes. I have never seen such abominations. They are unnatural. But, when they dug their way to the surface from your realm, swarmed over my friend, and dragged him back down into the tunnels I had no choice but to follow and try to save him."

Lithann heard many gasps and hushed whispers from the gathered crowd as she described the monsters and the attack on Jhonart. They definitely knew about these creatures. The judges remained stoic, however, so Lithann couldn't tell if the chimera were working for the dwarves or not.

"Are you saying we sent these rock...monsters to attack the wood elf realm?" asked the minister, venom dripping from each word.

Lithann didn't let on that she had noticed the misspoken word. They knew about the monsters and the minister seemed affronted by the notion that they would send them off to attack anyone. Lithann decided to play it innocent, because her only hope was that these creatures were a common enemy. If not, she was already dead and all of this was mere formality.

"I would never presume such a thing," she said. "I merely followed these creatures into a hole in the ground at the edge of the Straywood. I was as surprised to find myself in dwarven tunnels as you were to find me there. I had no idea your tunnels extended so far out from the Anvil Throne peaks. I apologize for trespassing."

It was a dangerous statement, but the judges' expressions were worth it. Plus, Lithann could see from the looks on the faces in the crowd that not all of them were against her any longer. Many were watching intently, their eyes no longer narrowed to slits of hatred, but open and questioning. She snuck a glance at Digur, the monk from the temple, and caught a hint of a smile peeking out from underneath his hood.

Now that she had let the dwarves know that she understood the significance of a long tunnel that led to the border between their lands, she offered the olive branch, before they decided to silence her, permanently. "If these foul monsters are also trespassing on your lands, perhaps we can help one another," she said. "If you help me find and save my friend, I will inform my people of this new enemy and we can help you fight them."

Lithann smiled at her maneuverings of the trial, but her happiness was short-lived.

"We do not require outside help with any internal Anvil Throne issues, child!" admonished the minister. "And as you have just admitted to your own crimes, I am prepared to pass judgment."

As the minister raised the rock, Lithann and another voice cried out at once.

"Wait!" said Lithann, not sure what more she could say, but needing to protest.

"Trial by combat!" yelled a male voice from the gallery. Lithann was certain it had been the scorched monk.

Before the minister could slam her rock down on the stone table, Lithann blurted out: "I demand trial by combat!"

The hushed silence that had gripped the crowd throughout the proceedings since Lithann had described the monsters erupted into a cacophony of shouts, cheers, and jeers. The crowd was definitely torn in their feelings, but whether that was over Lithann or something else, the elf was not sure.

The minister placed her rock back on the table and stood. The crowd immediately fell silent. "Are you certain you wish to accept the provisions of trial by combat?" she asked.

Lithann wasn't sure what she had gotten herself into here, but there was no going back. At the very least, they would expel her from the Anvil Throne for her so-called crimes, which would doom Jhonart.

"I accept," she said, her voice trembling just a bit.

"Done," said Minister Grimhammer. She raised her stone and banged it down on the table. The sound resonated throughout the chamber. "You will fight the champion of the Anvil Throne three hours hence."

The minister slammed the stone down again. "If you lose, you will be found guilty and your sentence will be carried out immediately." She pounded the table one more time. The entire chamber rumbled from the impact. "The sentence will be death!"

The entire crowd gasped in surprise at this statement. Afterward, some cheered, but the rest remained silent.

Lithann remained stoic, trying hard not to show her fear and surprise. After a moment, she spoke. "And if I win?" she asked as loud and clear and unwavering as she could.

"What?" asked the minister.

"What do I get if I win?" Lithann stared hard at the minister, as if willing arrows to fly from her eyes and impale the old dwarf.

"Why, you get your freedom, my child," she replied, smiling. "And an escort back to your lands."

Lithann took a step forward, which she realized was only a symbolic gesture at best, but it got all eyes in the room back on her.

"Not good enough," she said. "I came here to save my friend. If you send me back, you condemn him to death. That will not sit well with the council of Straywood."

The minister sat down and dropped her rock on the table with a thud. "What would you have us do, young one? Rouse an army to search for a single elf who most likely got lost on his own?"

"I will submit to your judgment peacefully if I lose," she said. "But should I win, I ask only for safe passage through your lands so I may continue to search for my friend and for any information you have on the monsters who abducted him."

The minister mulled that over for a moment. Lithann looked around the chamber and could see that she had won over a large portion of the crowd. That had to weigh on the minister's decision.

"I will stipulate," said the minister, "that should you survive the trial by combat, we will provide you aid in your search for your friend." She banged the rock on the table twice. "We are adjourned."

It was more than Lithann had hoped, which made her suspicious.

CHAPTER 5: TRIAL BY COMBAT

After the trial, Lithann's guards moved back into position around her and led her out toward the arena entrance. Never once did they attempt to take any of her visible weapons or search her for any hidden ones.

She felt certain these dwarves neither trusted her nor were they overly confident of their own battle prowess. It was a matter of numbers. She was deep in the Anvil Throne at this point. She might be able to kill a couple of guards—maybe even immobilize all four and make a run for it. But where could she go? How could she escape from hundreds, if not thousands of dwarves, most of whom would like nothing more than to see her dead?

She was completely alone, a strange elf in a strange, subterranean land. She'd be more frightened if it all didn't seem so familiar. Substitute these rocky tunnels for a canopy of trees, and the sullen, angry dwarves for indifferent, irritated elves, and her situation here was not much different from her formative years in the forest.

As the guards marched her into the tunnel outside the arena, Lithann caught a glimpse of Wiley skulking in the shadows near an intersection off to her left just as the guards turned to the right. She made a quick hand gesture to her pet as the guards hustled her along. When she glanced back again, Wiley had disappeared.

The forced march didn't last long, luckily, but it was certainly unpleasant. As the group moved through the tunnels, more and more dwarves appeared in the doorways and at intersections. Some simply stared at Lithann with either disgust lining their faces or hatred burning behind their eyes. Others jeered at her as she approached, spat at her as she went by, or threw rocks at her back.

The guards dissuaded the rock throwing somewhat, but did nothing about the rest. They finally came to a block of cells, which were little more than coffin-sized holes cut into the rock wall with iron bars that could be shackled in place over the opening.

After the commotion she had generated during the march, Lithann thought the cell was for her protection while she waited for the duel to begin. However, the truth soon became apparent when a parade of angry dwarves began to file past her cell, and the jeering, spitting, and rock throwing commenced once again.

The bars kept most of the rocks from actually hitting her, but could do nothing to ease the sting of angry dwarves who grabbed the bars of her cage and screamed things like, "monster," "demon," "leaf eater," or any number of even more vile names at her before spitting in her face.

She began to realize that the three-hour delay between the trial and the arena combat had nothing to do with the logistics of setting up the spectacle of the battle and everything to do with inflaming the racial fanaticism that not long ago had locked elves and dwarves into a generational war.

The ministers wanted Lithann to know she was far from home and had no friends here.

And then it happened. Amidst the long line of dwarves who came and screamed at Lithann, the robed monk she had met in the temple stepped up to her cell, the hood of his charred robe still hanging low over his brow. He lifted the hood a bit, caught her eye, and winked. He then screamed at her, not saying anything, just bellowing in rage as he practically put his face between the bars.

Lithann looked at him closely, leaning down in the confined space as much as she could. When her face came level with his, the dwarf whispered, "Swarm him!"

Lithann furrowed her eyebrows. "What?" she asked.

"Don't let the Grax set up his outposts," he whispered quickly. "Swarm him and beat him down before he can conjure the altar."

The next dwarf in line was pushing the robed monk away from the bars, yelling at him to move along.

"It's the only way!" screamed the monk as the line shoved him along down the tunnel. He dropped his hood over his face and skulked off.

Lithann tried to watch him as he left, but another dwarf had already stepped up to jeer at her, and decided to take advantage of her proximity to the bars by spitting in her eye. For the next couple of hours, Lithann ignored the jeering dwarves as best as she could and concentrated on what

Digur, the little robed monk, had told her.

At first she wasn't even sure if his ramblings held any real meaning. Who was she supposed to swarm? Was it this Grax, whatever that was? And how could she possibly swarm anyone or anything down here while completely surrounded and horribly outnumbered? And what was that about an altar? Did this Grax creature have something to with the little monk's burned-out temple?

As she pondered all these questions, the dwarves continued to stream past her cell. After she got spit in the face, she had leaned back in the tight crevice as best she could. She jammed her back up against the jagged rock wall and tried to keep her face far away from the bars, but that didn't stop them from screaming at her or spitting on her boots.

She tried to pay no attention to the taunts and rude dwarven gestures, most of which she didn't even understand—what possible meaning could be attached to someone poking their elbow with their thumb? It had to be a dwarf thing. She'd never seen an elf do that.

However, a couple of times the yelling penetrated her reverie. One dwarf yelled, "The Grax will grind you to gravel under his boots!" Another spit through the bars and yelled, "Give up now! An elf Beastmaster is no match for a dwarven Warlord."

Lithann loved watching duels, and never missed arena day in the forest. It was a festive time when she could forget about the loneliness of patrolling the border and soak up the excitement of the duels and the energy of the crowd. Even the disapproving, sidelong looks she received when her enthusiasm got the better of her never dampened her spirits much.

So, while she had never summoned the courage to enter the arena and test her skill against another mage, she had seen dozens of duels. Her parents had even taken her to Victoria once when she was young to see the championships.

A Warlord had won the day that year. He had been a human and not a dwarf, but Lithann remembered the duel clearly. She had never seen such enormous conjurations, and the Warlord had dotted the arena with them, creating building after building out of mana. His conjured city gave him total control of the arena in short order.

If this Grax was the champion she was about to duel, and he was a Warlord, then perhaps the little monk dwarf could be trusted—he had helped her during the trial. "Swarm him," he had said. She could do that. Yes she could. A plan began to form in Lithann's head, and if she was right about all of this, then perhaps a Beastmaster really could defeat a Warlord.

* * * * * *

Lithann arrived in the arena to a deafening chorus of boos, hisses, and jeering insults. Her guards stopped just inside the doorway, which had been carved into the corner of the rectangular arena, and unshackled her hands. Then they stepped back through the opening and took up position between her and freedom.

She had no intention of leaving, though. This battle was her only chance to continue searching for Jhonart, and she was determined to see it through.

When the boos and hisses from the gallery above her changed to cheers and applause, Lithann knew her opponent had arrived. She peered across the arena to size him up.

He certainly looked the part of Warlord. He wore a horned helm that framed a square-jawed face, plated armor engraved with glowing runes, and a large jade-headed hammer on his back.

But this Grax looked unlike most of the dwarves she'd seen so far. For one thing, he was nearly as tall as Lithann, standing a quarter of a meter taller than the guards standing behind him at the far exit. For another thing, his beard didn't flow down past his chest like most dwarves. He kept it close-cropped; just the opposite of his long hair, which flowed out from under his helm to drape across his shoulders and hang halfway down his back.

"Grax must mean mountain!" mused Lithann. "Let's see how the might of the mountain fares against the beasts of the forest."

The arena grew quiet and Lithann wondered if they had heard her boast, but she looked up to see Minister Grimhammer standing at her table.

"This duel between the elf interloper and the dwarven champion will decide the fate of our unwanted guest," said the minister. "Are you prepared for your trial by combat, little one?"

Lithann wanted to wipe the smug smile off the minister's face with an arrow to her forehead, but she simply nodded instead.

The minister banged her rock down hard on the stone table. "Begin!" she cried.

Lithann ran as far out into the middle of the arena as she could without losing her breath and then put her fingers to her mouth and whistled a long, high note that ascended in pitch at the end.

From behind her, she heard a commotion from the guards. She glanced back to see one sitting on his butt, still grasping his spear, which stuck straight up in the air. The other looked as if he wanted to run into the arena, but had thought better of it.

Wiley loped across the arena toward Lithann, her tongue lolling to one side out of her open, smiling mouth. Lithann patted her pet's head when she arrived next to her.

Turning back to see what the Warlord had done, Lithann was surprised to see him standing directly across from her in the center of the arena floor. Back at his doorway stood the Grax's first conjured outpost. Stacks of wooden planks and piles of cut stones had materialized out of nothing, while a wheel-powered crane came to life in the middle.

With the Grax so close, Lithann sent Wiley off to harass the Warlord while she began to conjure her creature swarm. First she took a moment to gather a cloud of mana to summon a large, green lizard called a tegu. The tegu opened its mouth and hissed at the Warlord, revealing a jagged row of sharp teeth and a long, snake-like tongue.

Then, using a trick Jhonart had taught her, Lithann snapped her fingers while summoning a small beast. Brownish mana flared around her finger-tips and shot out toward the stone floor beside her. A split-second later, a feral bobcat appeared as the mana dissipated. Its short, sharp claws pawed at the ground as it paced around on muscular legs.

Worried about Wiley, Lithann looked up to see how her pet was faring. The Warlord had conjured another outpost before the fox had gotten to him. It was a two-story, stone structure that looked like a small fort. Banners atop the fort even waved in some magical breeze that only they felt.

The Grax finished his conjuration and began to run off, just as he had after conjuring the construction yard. However, as he turned toward the back corner of the arena, Wiley nipped at his heels, catching him in the calf just below his armor. A trickle of blood began to flow down the champion's leg as he ran off.

Lithann commanded Wiley not to follow just yet and began preparing her next actions. The Warlord had conjured two outposts already and had ignored her pet when she bit into his leg, instead running off toward the corner of the arena. This quick build-up of conjured artifacts was just a means to an end, and he had yet to create an altar.

Lithann didn't know where all this conjuration was heading, but she knew she had to slow it down. She decided to continue building her army of forest creatures and then see what she could do about the stone building in front of her.

At the same time, the Warlord continued on to the corner of the arena where he conjured yet another outpost. This one looked like a log cabin with walls made from one-meter thick timbers. Perhaps it was another fort, but through the windows Lithann could see the interior walls were covered with weapons and armor. An armory, perhaps?

That was a question for later. Right now, Lithann had to concentrate on her own battle plan. She gathered enough mana to summon a timber wolf. As its thick, gray body materialized out of the ether, it growled a low menacing warning to the world. She then used her quick summoning trick to bring forth a mana-copy of Jhonart's pet—the Thunderift falcon.

Lithann had been so wrapped up in creating her army that she had failed to notice when a small, green-skinned humanoid creature emerged from the fort. It carried a pack filled with tools and stared, wide-eyed at her and Wiley.

Goblin! Lithann almost spat in disgust. They were filthy, horrible creatures with no respect at all for anything natural and unspoiled. However, she had bigger concerns than one single goblin at the moment. The stone fort was apparently a barracks, and had deployed the foul creature. Lithann knew she needed to maintain numerical superiority, so the barracks had to go.

She commanded Wiley, the tegu, and the bobcat to ignore the goblin and attack the barracks instead. Wiley looked at the stone structure and then looked back at Lithann. She swore the fox raised one eyebrow at her, as if to say, "You want me to bite what?" But Lithann knew that while conjured structures were as solid as any stone structure or as tough as real tree trunks, they still could be destroyed.

Wiley set her back paws against the stone floor and lunged at the barracks with her jaws wide open. She took a mighty bite out of the cornerstone, which melted into wisps of green energy in her mouth. The bobcat charged from Lithann's side and swiped at the wall next to the fort's door, gouging a trio of furrows into the wall that seemed to go all the way through. The tegu followed closely behind the bobcat, but veered off to the corner opposite Wiley before closing its massive jaws around a huge slab of stone jutting out from the base of the structure.

After the trio of attacks, the entire front of the barracks looked like it was about ready to fall over. Both of its cornerstones were severely weakened, and the front wall had been sliced open.

Lithann was happy with the results, but she also felt quite weary all of a sudden. She had never summoned and controlled so many creatures this fast before. Breathing heavily, she glanced once more at the Warlord and noticed that his helm had begun to glow with a bluish miasma of mana encircling it.

The Grax had placed some sort of incantation on his helm while she was watching her animals attack his barracks, but she hadn't seen him cast it, so had no idea what it might be. With her own mana reserves low, and now facing an opponent with an unknown spell stored in his helm, Lithann decided she'd better start pacing herself a bit and pay more attention to the Warlord moving forward.

As Lithann prepared a single spell, another goblin appeared at the door to the fort. It began picking through the pack of tools on its back as it smirked an evil little smile at Lithann.

Peering behind the barracks, Lithann watched the Warlord in the corner, trying to see what he had planned for her next. He hadn't moved from beside the wooden armory. Instead, he began channeling mossy green mana into an open area dead center between the three outposts he'd already conjured.

Once the mana coalesced, streams of energy snaked out from all three outposts and shot a beam of mana into the head of the statue. Lithann recognized the altar and this affect. The human Warlord she'd seen in Victoria had also conjured this artifact. She had to act fast before the energy from the outposts brought the legendary Talos to life atop the altar. He would wreak havoc on her army.

Luckily, she was prepared to go on the offensive now. As Lithann strode toward the barracks, she placed an enchantment on Wiley and commanded her pet to attack the Warlord. The spell gave her fox the savagery of a lion. Wiley bolted across the arena toward the corner and lunged at the Grax, knocking the giant dwarf back a step as she dug her now ten-centimeter-long fangs into his neck.

A great gout of blood erupted from the exposed flesh just above his plated armor making the entire crowd gasp in surprise and horror. Lithann felt certain they'd never seen their champion suffer such a ferocious attack.

Wiley landed beside the Warlord, blood dripping from her jaws. Her tongue licked the red liquid away from around her mouth before lolling back to one side in a look that Lithann swore was a contented smile.

That smile didn't last long, however. The Warlord wiped blood from the long, jagged rip in his flesh and glared at the tiny fox at his feet. In one, smooth motion, he grabbed the jade-headed hammer from his back and swung it down with all his might toward the fox's head. A bright rune flashed on the green head as it streaked down toward her pet and for a brief second, Lithann swore she saw the blunt end of the hammer elongate into a point.

The hammer smashed into Wiley's head with such force it split it open and drove the fox's smiling snout down into the rock floor. Blood and brains sprayed across the floor from the impact and Wiley lay motionless in a growing crimson pool.

Lithann screamed and blood rushed to her face. She balled her hands into fists and wanted nothing more than to run to her pet and hold her as she died. No, that was wrong. She did want one thing more than that. She wanted the Warlord to pay. She wanted him to suffer. She wanted him to lose!

With a strength of will unlike any she had ever summoned before in her life, Lithann looked away from her dead pet and concentrated on the tasks at hand. She needed to take everything the Warlord had created away from him, and then she needed to crush him.

She glanced back at the barracks and noticed a new creature had emerged sometime in that last few moments. It had green skin like the goblins, but stood at least two meters tall. Lithann had never seen one before, but she knew this to be an orc, one of the most feared monstrous races in Etheria. It wore long, studded leather armor and a horned helm much like the Warlord's. It snapped the barbed whip in its hand, making the tiny goblins jump and salute at the same time.

Lithann ignored the massive orc, and commanded her falcon, bobcat, and lizard to destroy the barracks, while sending the wolf off to harry the Grax and make sure he couldn't escape the corner of the arena. As her creatures attacked the stone structure, she watched as the Warlord's first goblin vainly pounded a new support block into place under the watchful eye of the orc with the whip.

A moment later, as the tegu's mouth ripped the other cornerstone out completely, the bobcat slashed a small hole into the front wall, and the falcon pecked right through the new support, the goblin's work was completely undone, and the entire structure collapsed into a cloud of mana.

The beam of energy connecting the barracks to the other two outposts faltered and faded, followed quickly by the beams emanating from the other outposts. The air around Talos dimmed as the mana stopped flowing around his head.

The Grax growled when his barracks crumbled and the energy stopped flowing toward the altar. Lithann didn't even smile as she calmly pulled the bow off her back, nocked an arrow, and pulled the string taut. She loosed the arrow and watched it fly straight and true, burying itself in the temple of one of the Warlord's goblins. The disgusting green creature dropped to the floor immediately and dissolved away, leaving her arrow clattering on the stone floor.

"You can't hide in the corner forever," she called out at him. "Are you afraid of a few woodland critters and a girl with a bow? Or are we going to fight, you and I?"

The Warlord's grumble turned into a bellow of rage. He uttered a command word that made his helm glow and strode purposefully toward Lithann's wolf. Before her creature could even react, the Grax swung his mighty hammer not once, but twice, through the air.

The first swing caught the wolf in the right ear. A great gout of blood sprayed from the wolf's head. Then he brought the hammer swinging back impossibly fast, cracking the beast in the chest. Even from where she stood, Lithann could hear the wolf's ribs crack from the impact.

Amazingly, though, the wolf still stood in front of the Warlord, if a bit shakily, after the flurry. It growled menacingly, awaiting its master's commands. The Warlord, stunned that the wolf could withstand two mighty blows from his hammer, took a step back.

For the first time in the fight, Lithann thought she saw a glimmer of doubt cross the Grax's face like a dark cloud crossing in front of the sun. If he knew what Lithann had planned for him, though, that cloud would have been more like a storm front blotting out the sky from horizon to horizon.

Her taunt had brought the Warlord into range of all her creatures, so she ordered them to attack. The wolf repaid the double blows it had received with a ferocious bite to the Warlord's thigh that ripped a hand-sized chunk of flesh from his upper leg.

The bobcat charged at the Grax, leaping at the last moment and slicing open the dwarf's chest, right through his armor. A stream of blood trickled down the plates and dripped on the stone floor.

The falcon dove out of the air and pecked at his face, ripping out a large chunk of the Grax's nose and swallowing it. The lizard then lumbered up and bit the Warlord, sinking its slathering jaws into the soft flesh of the dwarf's backside.

She gathered all of her available mana, even tapping into the moonglow amulet around her neck for some added energy, and summoned one of her favorite creatures next to her beloved Wiley.

A muddy cloud of mana began to take shape next to Lithann, becoming a black panther with eyes as yellow as the sun and fur as black as midnight. "Hello, Cervere," said Lithann to the legendary cat. "I have a dwarven morsel for you."

Before she could command the forest shadow to attack, though, the Grax's last goblin moved toward Lithann. She paid no attention to it because she knew it could do nothing of any consequence at this point. In her mind, the duel was basically over. However, it did surprise her by building a small, wooden outpost right next to her.

The tall wooden structure materialized beside her and the energy lines reconnected with the statue of Talos. However, as the altar began to glow near the edge of the arena, Lithann simply stared at the Warlord and began preparing the last two spells she would need to finish this fight.

First, she gathered enough mana in her hands to cast a quick binding spell. She tossed the ball of mana at the Warlord where it encircled him and solidified into a tangle of vines that twisted and tightened around his legs, holding him in place.

"Can't have you running off, now can I?" she said as she prepared her next spell.

The Grax stared silently at his cage and responded only by uttering the command to activate the spell stored in his helm.

Lithann knew he would target the wolf again, so she commanded it to attack before the Warlord could use his hammer to inflict another flurry of blows on the wolf. It lunged and bit him in the other thigh, tearing another chunk of flesh out of the dwarven champion. He now bled from multiple wounds across his body.

The Warlord simply smiled as another bluish glow enveloped him. Lithann hadn't seen the Grax cast the spell, though, so she looked around to see where the incantation had come from. Wisps of blue mana hung in the air between the Warlord and the whip-wielding orc that had emerged from the barracks a few moments before.

Lithann had not realized the huge, green creature was a familiar, but she had no time to second-guess herself now. The Grax practically shimmered in the dim light of the arena, either from the energy of two spells surrounding his body or from the speed of his movements.

The Warlord swung his mighty hammer in a great circle around himself, slamming it in quick succession against the heads of all three animals within striking distance. He caught the lizard in the side of the head, but the blow glanced off its thick hide, leaving little but a trickle of blood behind.

The hammer then hit the bobcat squarely in the snout. Blood spewed from its nostrils, and it looked a bit dazed, but it shook its head clear and growled at the Warlord. It had survived.

The wolf took the third hit directly to its front-right leg, which snapped. The beast was not dead, but it limped back a few steps after the attack, and howled in pain.

However, the Warlord wasn't done. The blazing speed he'd gained from the two incantations gave him one final attack against Lithann's animals. He aimed it at the bobcat, bringing the hammer down in an overhand attack that looked as if it would take the bobcat's head clean off at the neck. The quick beast dodged out of the path just before the blow landed, though, barely escaping death.

In the aftermath of the stunning, quadruple attack, nothing at all had changed, however, and Lithann knew it was now truly over.

"My turn," she said. She cast her final spell. Raising her hands toward the stone ceiling high above, she began channeling mana through her fingertips as she threw her head back and howled! The mana streamed from her hands and flew around the arena as the echo of her howling bounced from wall to wall.

As the streaming mana touched her creatures, they began to howl as well. The combined roar of howls enveloped the room and hushed the crowd. Then, all went completely silent as Lithann and the creatures stopped howling at the same time.

A moment later, Lithann cried, "Attack!"

Empowered by her call of the wild, all of her creatures attacked the Warlord with such savagery that he didn't stand a chance of surviving.

The bobcat sliced razor-sharp claws across the Warlord's torso, tearing a huge gash in his stomach. The tegu lizard tore another, larger chunk of flesh out of his backside, while the falcon dove from the sky and gouged at one of the Grax's eyes, plucking it clean out of its socket.

Lithann glanced down at Cervere just in time to see it take off at top speed toward the tangled Warlord. Its pitch-black fur practically drank in the light from the torches hanging on the wall, making it almost impossible to see as it ran, but a moment later it pounced on the Warlord, wrapping its huge jaws around his neck and closing like a vise. At the same time, the shadow panther's claws raked at the Grax's face, leaving three, long trails of blood from the edge of his helmet down his cheeks to his square jaw.

As ferocious as all of these attacks had been, the Warlord still stood. Blood streamed from his face, chest, stomach, and legs, leaving a growing puddle of viscous, red goo at his feet, but he remained standing.

Lithann stared at the bloody champion for one long moment before grabbing an arrow from her quiver and nocking it on her bowstring. She practically caressed the taut string before pulling it back and bending the re-curved hunting bow to its limit.

She sighted down the shaft, pulled and released in a single, smooth motion. The arrow flew, splitting the silence in the arena with the barest whistle as it sped through the air and pierced the Warlord through the neck.

As he fell, the vines entangling his legs splintered and frayed, unable to keep his dead weight upright. With a thud, the lifeless body of the dwarven champion crumpled to the floor as all of his conjurations and his lone summoned creature dissolved into clouds of mana and began to dissipate.

CHAPTER 6: TUNNELS AND TALES

The stunned silence that had permeated the crowd while Lithann's creatures ripped the dwarven champion apart erupted into total chaos.

Most of the crowd screamed in horror or yelled death threats down at Lithann, while a sizeable minority began to clap and cheer. Above the tumult, Lithann could barely hear Minister Grimhammer calling for silence as she banged her rock down on the table over and over and over again.

Lithann dismissed her creatures and walked toward the back corner of the arena where the mangled body of Wiley still lay in a pool of blood. Behind her, healers rushed to the bloody body of the Grax, who had sprawled into a heap within his own crimson pool after Lithann's tangle vines had disappeared.

As Lithann knelt down beside her dead pet, she could hear the Minister's voice rising above the din overhead. "Stop her!" she yelled. "Restrain that elf! Silence! Order! I will have order in this arena!"

Lithann avoided looking at Wiley's crushed head and the spray of brain matter that she knew to have stained the stone floor. She did not want that image burned into her memory forever. The rest of her fox—her friend—looked almost peaceful, as if she could maybe just be sleeping.

With the guards quickly approaching her from the far end of the arena, Lithann gathered a couple of handfuls of dark blue energy in her palms. She spoke the incantation quickly, fearing the guards would prevent her from finishing, and never let her near her pet again. But incantations can't be rushed. The words must all be spoken properly. The hand motions must all be coordinated with the incantation just so.

Lithann forced her mind to concentrate on the spell and block out all the extraneous distractions. One by one, the bits of commotion around her disappeared: the guards tromping up behind her, the healers casting spells over the still form of the Grax, the crowd's cheers and jeers, and the minister's incessant rock pounding and commanding for attention.

The only thing that remained in Lithann's world was her pet and her spell.

The guards grabbed her from behind and pulled her to her feet just as she completed the last syllable of the incantation and finished the final hand gesture. She allowed them to pull her back away from Wiley, still training her eyes on the fox's body and not her head.

The dwarven guards dragged Lithann back to the center of the arena, her feet leaving a double trail of blood across the stone floor.

She glanced over at the Grax, who was standing, a bit unsteadily, next to the healers. He caught her eye and nodded at her before allowing the healers to lead him out of the arena. Lithann nodded back as he limped away. They were no longer mortal enemies, nor even two people caught up in racial hatred. They were simply two dueling mages showing respect for one another.

Above Lithann, Minister Grimhammer had finally quieted the crowd with the constant banging of her stone of command. The dour minister stared down at Lithann, her face filled with silent rage. No sign of the respect her champion had just showed Lithann could ever cross that deeply-lined face.

"Well, little one, it seems you have defeated our champion," said the minister.

"Yes, I have," said Lithann, feeling more confidence in herself than she had ever felt before. "I have won my trial by combat and I demand you provide the assistance you promised."

Minister Grimhammer smiled; an expression that made Lithann go cold inside. "You didn't let me finish," she said. "You prevailed to be sure, but you also cheated, and for that you will be banished from our kingdom."

The crowd reacted even before Lithann. Cheers and applause ringed the arena, but she could hear a few boos and jeers as well. She had won over part of the crowd, but not all.

Lithann willed herself to remain calm. She had often been told that she allowed her emotions to rule her interactions with others, and it always put people off. "I won this duel fairly," she said in a calm voice that belied the turmoil raging beneath her face. "Ask your own champion. I am certain he will claim no foul in his defeat."

"You brought a companion in with you to the arena," said Grimhammer, pointing at the bloody corner.

Lithann didn't want to look over at her dead pet again, but couldn't help herself. What she saw made her heart almost leap out of her chest. Sitting there, tongue lolling out the side of her short snout, sat Wiley, whole and healthy.

Grimhammer continued, but Lithann barely heard her. "Outside help is strictly against the rules," she said. "Therefore, I declare your victory forfeit, and your original sentence reinstated." The booing in the arena grew louder and did not stop even after Minister Grimhammer banged her stone five, six, seven times.

Lithann smiled, despite her reversal of fortune. Wiley was alive and the dwarves were voicing their displeasure with Grimhammer. The minister's eyes darted back and forth at the crowd. Not everyone was yelling, but there were no longer any cheers for her actions. And, try as she might to regain control with her rock, she could not.

Finally she sighed and placed her stone down on the table. "However!" she yelled above the din. "However," she tried again and the jeers abated a bit. "Never let it be said that the Anvil Throne is not a compassionate kingdom."

The crowd quieted, waiting to see what she would say next. "We shall provide assistance in your search, little one," she said. "You will be escorted to the farthest reaches of our kingdom and set free. So long as you do not trespass within our borders again, you will be unharmed. The assistance we shall provide is your life!"

"But—" started Lithann.

"The creatures you seek are called rock devils," said the minister. "They do not dwell in our kingdom and they are not our minions. You are free to search for them, but do not enter the kingdom of the Anvil Throne again, or your life will be forfeit."

She banged her stone of command twice quickly, and then turned and left the arena. There was, apparently no appeal Lithann could make.

*　　*　　*　　*　　*　　*

Lithann's emotions churned inside her as the guards marched her back through the dwarven tunnels. She felt elated at the sound of Wiley padding along behind her. Nothing had ever made her as happy as seeing her pet's smiling, panting face looking at her with unconditional love sparkling behind her eyes.

But rage welled up inside Lithann as well. When she closed her eyes she could see the smug, smiling face of Minister Grimhammer and hear her grating voice calling her "little one" as she banished her back to the dark.

A hopelessness and a loneliness like she had never felt before began to descend around Lithann as the guards passed the last of the candlelit chambers and the tunnels darkened around her. She could have commanded her amulet to glow, but the darkness surrounding her matched the blackness of her mood. She craved the light, but felt like she didn't deserve it.

How could she have risen so far and defeated the Grax only to be sent out into the wilderness...the tunnels...alone? How could she enjoy the arena so much—even the dwarven arena—only to be told she didn't deserve to be there? She hated being alone, but she had been told over and over throughout her life that she simply didn't belong, didn't fit in, didn't know to act in polite society.

Wiley must have sensed her dark mood because she pranced up beside her in the darkness and jumped and licked at her bound hands.

"Tell that thing to behave or we'll skewer it," said one of the guards.

Another guard piped up. "Leave her alone, Grungle," he said. "The fox isn't doing anything wrong."

"Thank you," said Lithann to the second dwarf.

"We're almost to the edge of the Anvil Throne lands," said the kind dwarf. "It's just past the temple up ahead."

Lithann saw the light and knew where she was—back to where it had all started. A few moments later, the kind guard unshackled her and, in the dim light coming from the temple chamber, pointed on down the tunnel. "You can find your way out down that way," he said. "Good luck!"

"Damned elf lover!" grumbled Grungle, looking at the other dwarf. "Get out, girl, and don't come back."

"You're just sore because when you fought the Grax, you didn't so much as lay a hand on him before he cut you down," said the kind dwarf as he shoved Grungle back down the tunnel the way they had come.

Lithann stood in the dim light a dozen meters past the entrance to the temple for a minute trying to decide what to do. She wasn't ready to give up on finding Jhonart, but the chimerical creatures now had a several hour head start on her and she had no idea where they had gone.

If Minister Grimhammer was to be believed, they weren't anywhere in the Anvil Throne tunnels. Had she missed something? She decided she would have to backtrack all the way to the hole and start over.

She scratched Wiley between her ears and said, "Come on, girl. Let's go back to the beginning and try again." She turned and began walking down the long, dark tunnel alone with her thoughts and her pet.

"I know where the rock devils took your friend," said a low, soft, yet distinctly dwarven voice from behind her.

She turned back, expecting to see the kind guard, but instead saw the little monk in the robes poking his head out of the temple.

"What?" she asked.

He stepped out of the temple into the tunnel. The light from the chamber lit only part of his body, while the rest was hidden in shadow, making him look like only half a dwarf.

"The creatures who abducted your friend," he said slowly, as if that would help her understand. "We call them rock devils. I can help you find them. I—"

He hesitated a moment and took a deep breath before continuing. "I will help you find them. I will help you save your friend."

"Why would you do that?" asked Lithann. She found it hard to trust the little dwarf despite the help he'd provided twice before. It all could be some convoluted plan by Minister Grimhammer to lure her back to her death.

"Because we have common enemies," said the dwarf.

"Those...rock devils?" asked Lithann. She began to move back toward the door to see him a little better. With the dark covering half his face, she couldn't tell if he was earnest or duplicitous.

"Them, yes." he said, "Definitely! But also Minister Grimhammer!"

"The minister is your enemy?" asked Lithann as she took another step forward. She had almost returned to the pool of light that spilled out of the temple chamber.

"Stop!" yelled the dwarf. "Don't take another step!"

Lithann halted. "Why?" she asked. "What's wrong?"

"If you step into the light, you will once again be inside Anvil Throne territory," he said. "I assure you they are still watching you."

He looked around furtively, and his hand twitched a bit as he wiped a bead of sweat off his temple.

"In fact, I should not be seen talking with you any longer," he continued. "Go down this tunnel and wait for me past the intersection. I will come to you in a little while once the guards leave the area."

"I won't wait long," said Lithann. "I lost hours of search time while stuck in a cage." The statement practically dripped with venom.

"It won't be long," he said. "I promise. After you disappear around the corner, they will lose interest quickly. Now, go!"

Lithann turned and walked down the tunnel, keeping one hand on the wall to guide her so she could move more quickly in the dark.

As she walked away, she heard the little dwarven monk yell, much louder than he truly needed for her to hear him, "And don't come back, elf scum!"

*   *   *   *   *   *

Digur walked back into the temple and planned his next actions. He didn't really want to do this, but he felt he had no choice. Minister Grimhammer had plunged the Anvil Throne's metaphorical head under a proverbial boulder.

No one would listen to him now that he'd been defeated, and his banishment meant he couldn't even talk to those who felt, like he did, that walling off the rock devils wouldn't stop their incursions, wouldn't end the bloodshed.

Even this elf's story of the rock devils tunneling all the way to the surface world had not swayed the ministers. How could they not see that this danger was too big for one race—even the mighty Anvil Throne dwarves—to overcome alone?

After several long minutes, Digur channeled a sizable amount of mana into his hands and summoned an invisible stalker, a creature of pure energy. The Forcemaster watched the shimmering, blue biped flex the sinewy muscles in its long, strong arms and thick legs, as if removing the kinks after a long sleep.

A ring of blue spikes jutted up from its temple, encircling the creature's head like a crown. As it stared down at Digur waiting for a command, the tentacles at its jaw twisted and turned like a tangle of snakes.

Digur could see the stalker because he had summoned it, but no one else would ever know it was there unless it attacked. With a mental command, Digur sent the beast down the hall toward the guards to check on their attentiveness.

He concentrated his mind on the stalker as it left the temple chamber so he could see the world through the stalker's eyes. It moved down the tunnel silently. Through its eyes, the pitch-black tunnel appeared lit by a pale blue light. When it reached the guards, they also seemed to be outlined in blue light, looking much like the stalker looked to Digur.

He could see they were talking and not paying attention to the tunnel. They would glance down toward the temple periodically, however, so Digur didn't dare leave just yet.

He sent the stalker past the guards and around the corner. A bead of sweat trickled down Digur's nose as the strain of maintaining control on the stalker began to wear on him. He moved to the doorway to be ready for the next part, and then sent an attack command to the stalker.

The beast gouged a large chunk of rock out of the tunnel wall with its powerful claws and let it crash to the stone floor. The sound echoed down the hallway.

"What in Infernia was that?" said one of the guards.

"What's that blue glow?" said the other.

Digur stepped out of the temple, sweat now streaming down his cheeks and mingling with his beard. Without looking back, he began to move down the tunnel as quickly and silently as he could while maintaining his stalker. He commanded it to tear another chunk of rock out of the wall and fling it at the corner.

As the rock smashed into the wall behind him, Digur heard the first guard say, "Come on! We better check this out!" As the sound of two sets of armored feet echoed down the tunnel behind him, Digur dismissed the invisible stalker and walked into the darkness, away from his home.

*   *   *   *   *   *

Lithann waited in the dark tunnel a dozen meters or so past the intersection. She held her moonglow amulet cupped in the palm of one hand so it would illuminate the area around her while preventing the light from spilling out past the corner where it might be seen by the guards down the long tunnel. She idly scratched Wiley between the ears with her other hand as she waited.

As the minutes stretched out, she began to feel foolish for waiting at all for the little dwarf. But he had helped her in the arena, and if his offer to guide her to the rock devils was genuine, she had to take a chance. She owed it to Jhonart.

After what seemed an eternity, she heard faint footsteps coming toward her, and the little dwarf appeared in the small pool of light.

"What took you so long?" she asked, still not sure whether or not she could trust him.

"I had to distract the guards so they wouldn't see me follow you," he replied. "Come, we should move off from here in case they decide to come check on you."

He walked past Lithann and disappeared into the darkness, heading down the tunnel that led straight back to the hole.

"Wait!" called Lithann as she let the moonglow pendant fall back between her breasts on its chain. The unfettered light illuminated an arc of the tunnel in front of her as she ran to catch up with the dwarf. Wiley padded along beside her.

"Stop!" she said as she caught up with the dwarf. She grabbed his shoulder and turned him around. "That takes us back to the rock devil hole I climbed down. I thought you were going to take me to their lair, not return me to the surface."

"Listen, elf," he said, sternly. "You know nothing about these tunnels." He stopped, took a breath, and began again, softening his tone. "What was your name?"

"I am Lithann," she said. "And I promise you I will not leave the darkness without my friend."

"Good," he said. "I'm glad to hear the determination in your voice." He smiled up at her, which made the beard hairs around his mouth twitch a bit. "My name is Digur, and I know these tunnels like the back of my hand. I should. I built most of them."

"So, where are you taking me, Digur?" asked Lithann, "because I came down this tunnel earlier and there are no turns, no openings, nothing between us and that damned hole."

"It's easier if I just show you," he said. "Come. It's not far."

Digur headed down the tunnel ahead of Lithann. She had to follow or lose him in the darkness past the light of her amulet. After a short time, he stopped, turned to the side wall, and began running his hand along it, slowly, like he was looking for something.

"Ahh," he said. "Here we go."

To Lithann, the wall in front of Digur looked the same as the surrounding wall. Beside her, Wiley was practically vibrating from excitement. Small whimpers escaped her lips and she pawed at Lithann's leg. Lithann looked back and forth between Digur and Wiley.

"Shine your light up near the ceiling," said Digur, pointing.

She grabbed her amulet and tilted it so the light reached the ceiling. At the intersection of wall and ceiling she saw a small opening, just big enough for a single elf, dwarf, or rock devil to crawl through.

"How did I miss that?" she asked. "I mean I was walking in the dark at this point, but Wiley should have noticed."

"Looks like she did," said Digur, pointing at the fox.

With a mighty leap, Wiley jumped up, scrabbled at the wall for a moment and caught the lip of the opening with her front paws. She pulled herself in and then turned around and stared down at the two of them, her tongue lolling to one side.

"So that's where you disappeared to," said Lithann. She looked back at Digur "How did you know where to look?"

"We walled up a much bigger rock devil tunnel here a few weeks back," he said. "But they're getting smarter. That small access tunnel up there might have gone unnoticed for months if you hadn't followed your friend down their hole. And who knows how many more would have been killed."

Digur knelt on all fours next to the wall and looked up at Lithann. "Climb on," he said. "I'll help you up and then you can pull me up behind you."

Lithann looked at the surrounding wall again and marveled once again at the dwarves' ability to create these tunnels. Then she climbed on top of Digur and pulled herself into the hole.

A moment later, she and Digur were crawling through the cramped passage. Wiley padded on ahead, her head bowed slightly to avoid hitting the top of the low tunnel. The grooves in the walls of the circular passage were identical to those she'd seen in the hole Jhonart had fallen into. This was definitely a rock devil tunnel.

Lithann could hear Digur crawling through behind her. The thought of being in such a vulnerable position ahead of a dwarf would have terrified her a while ago, but Digur was different from every dwarf she had ever met. Still she wanted to be out of this narrow space as quickly as possible.

"How far does this go?" she asked, trying to keep her voice from trembling.

"About fifty meters," said Digur. "We filled in their large tunnel with the hardest rock we have, and it hardly slowed them down. I told the minister we couldn't contain them, but she didn't listen."

"How long have you known about the rock devils?" asked Lithann. Fifty meters didn't seem like a long way, but crawling that distance in these cramped quarters was already making her muscles ache.

For a moment, the only sound in the tight passage was the scraping of legs and hands and paws against stone as the trio inched forward.

"I don't really like to talk about it," said Digur finally, quietly.

Lithann pressed him. "I need to know everything you know," she said. "To have any chance of saving Jhonart, I need to learn as much as I can about the rock devils."

"It's hard," said Digur. "Painful."

Lithann reached a small chamber in the narrow passage. It was little more than widened section of tunnel, but it allowed her to sit up and turn around. She needed a break and a chance to stretch her legs, so she turned around and faced Digur, who had followed her into the chamber.

"You lost people, didn't you?" she asked.

Digur, now bathed in the light of her moonglow amulet, only nodded.

"Friends? Family?" Lithann reached out and laid her hand on the dwarf's arm.

"My brother," said Digur.

"I'm so sorry," said Lithann. Wiley padded up beside her and then, instinctively, took two more steps and began licking Digur's hand.

He patted her head and scratched behind her ears before talking again. "We dug too deep," he said. "My brother and I led the construction crew. We were tasked with creating a whole new level to the great city. We'd designed the entire sector. It was going to be glorious.

"We planned to dig out several huge chambers with openings at multiple levels connected by stone bridges that would house hundreds of multi-chambered dwellings with running water, radiant heating, and windows that looked out on the communal chambers.

"We also designed a central plaza for mass gatherings. The plaza would be dotted with statues, fountains, and moss gardens. We devoted one whole wall of the chamber to a massive staircase that led to the new, six-story-tall imperial mansion. Dozens of windows and three huge balconies would overlook the plaza..."

Digur trailed off. Lithann allowed him a few minutes with his thoughts before prodding him, gently, to continue.

"What happened?" she asked, softly.

After another minute, Digur looked up at Lithann again. She could see two tears trailing down his cheeks from moist eyes.

"My brother and I led a preliminary digging team down into the depths beneath the lowest levels of the dwarven kingdom," he said. "We were going to dig all the connecting tunnels before enlarging the caverns we needed for the residences and the imperial plaza."

He wiped the tears away with the back of his hands and cleared his throat. "We had to go deep, you see. The design called for multiple, forty-meter-tall chambers, so we had to dig down five times that far to provide stability between levels."

"And you found the rock devils when you got down there?" asked Lithann. She hadn't moved her hand from the back of the dwarf's arm. Wiley had lain down between the two mages and looked from one to the other as they spoke.

"More like they found us," said Digur. "We broke through into a series of tunnels none of us knew existed. They had all been dug out like these." Digur pointed to the gouged walls around them. "But they were three meters in diameter, and the system of tunnels was incredibly intricate."

"You wandered through the rock devil realm?" asked Lithann.

"They didn't know we were there at first," said Digur. "I guess we had broken through in an unused area. But once one of them saw us, it was like the entire race of the buggers knew we were there."

Digur shook his head at the memory. "We fought and killed the first one we saw," he said. "It didn't even have time to warn the others, but somehow they all knew. Soon we were swarmed, and there was nothing we could do but run.

"One by one, our digging team was picked off. My brother, Dargur, and I could hear their screams behind us. A single rock devil is not all that formidable, but a hundred, all moving in coordinated attacks, is a terrible sight to behold."

Digur shuddered at the memory. "I saw ten rock devils dive from the walls onto one of our diggers, slamming into him one after another without getting in each other's way. He was dead in seconds, caught in a whirlwind of slashing claws and clacking mandibles. It was like watching startled bats fly past—only bats won't leave your body sliced into bits and pieces no bigger than a fist."

Digur stared at Wiley for a long moment before continuing. "I tried to turn back and help our crew, but Dargur grabbed my shoulders and pushed me ahead of him. He said, 'We have to escape, brother. We must warn the ministers.' So, we ran and we didn't look back.

"Not long after, I glanced back and realized that Dargur and I were the last ones left alive from our original group of two dozen. And these weren't your average diggers. Each was an accomplished mage, handpicked by Dargur and me. They were the best of the best, and the rock devils ripped them all apart like they were first-year apprentices.

"Dargur and I could see our access tunnel ahead of us, but we also saw another horde of rock devils heading at us from the other side of the opening. They moved like beetles, swarming across every surface, making the rock wall look like a living, breathing thing."

"You made it into the tunnel and your brother didn't?" asked Lithann in a small, soft voice.

Digur shook his head. "No," he said. "Dargur was ahead of me at that point. He could always beat me in a race. He could have made it into the access tunnel easily before the horde arrived, but there was no way I was going to make it in time."

Digur took a long, deep breath and dropped his head down so far that his beard pooled on the stone floor of the tunnel like a coil of rope.

"He could have made it," he said finally. "But if we didn't wall off that tunnel, they would have swarmed us both before I could make it inside. I knew it. He knew it."

"He sacrificed himself for you?" asked Lithann, astounded. She knew it to be true, but the thought of dwarves—mortal enemies of her race for as long as she could remember—having the capacity for self-sacrifice ran afoul of everything she had ever been taught.

"He could have saved himself," said Digur. His words came haltingly now as he choked back the tears. "He should have saved himself and left me behind. But he didn't.

"Dargur ran past the access tunnel and brought down a hail of stones above the approaching horde to slow them down. I made it to the entrance and yelled at him. 'Come on!' I screamed. 'I'm in! Let's go!' He glanced back at me, nodded his head, and placed a wall of stone over the entrance, blocking me behind it—blocking his path to freedom."

CHAPTER 7: DOWN THE SHAFT

"There was nothing you could do," said Lithann, trying to comfort the dwarf. He looked so small and alone to her at that moment, sitting with his head bowed, his body slumped over.

"Yes, there was," said Digur. He straightened up and looked steadily at Lithann, his eyes dry and penetrating now, a look of determination replacing the sadness. "I could have honored his sacrifice by convincing the ministers to do anything and everything in their power to deal with the rock devils."

He motioned Lithann to continue down the tunnel. She turned and hunched over onto her hands and knees again to continue their long crawl.

"Is that why you agreed to come with me?" she asked as she moved ahead.

"Partly," said Digur. She could hear him following her again. "But also because I have to do something, even if the ministers won't. Plus, I see how much you care for your friend; it's as much as I loved my brother."

Lithann let all of that sink in. "Did the ministers do nothing at all?" she asked.

"Oh, at first, they sent war parties down there," he said. "I even led several forays into the rock devil tunnels. But we suffered massive casualties every time, and no matter how many rock devils we killed, more spilled out of the walls. There never seemed to be any end to them."

They moved along in silence for a bit. The going was still slow and Lithann calculated that they were only three-quarters of the way through the tunnel.

"After a half-dozen failed attacks on the rock devils," continued Digur, "the ministers called for the closure of all tunnels leading down to their domain."

"Forgive me for saying this," said Lithann. She had come to a stop and turned her head and amulet back toward Digur to look at him. "That seems sensible. In fact, I'm starting to wonder if there's any chance we can survive down there, let alone help Jhonart...if he's even still alive."

"The only sensible course against the rock devils is to wipe them out," said Digur. "I argued with the ministers that we should seek help from the other races to do just that. If we ignore them, they *will* overrun us all eventually—dwarves, elves, humans—everyone."

"Maybe I should just return to my people and tell them about the rock devils," said Lithann. Self-doubt threatened to stifle the passion she'd had earlier during the trial and the duel. "There's no sense in both of us dying down there."

"Your friend is still alive," said Digur. "And I believe we can reach him. Many of my people have also been captured since we began fighting the rock devils. One—a female Warlord—survived and returned home."

"What happened to her?" asked Lithann. "How did she escape?"

"That's a story for another time," said Digur, motioning for Lithann to keep moving. "I'll say this, though. Most everyone in the Anvil Throne thinks the ordeal drove her mad. Nobody actually believed her story. It was too crazy."

"But you did, didn't you?" asked Lithann as she began crawling forward again. She tried to push her self-doubt back where it normally resided: next to her loneliness, deep down in her gut.

"Yes," said Digur. "Yes, I did. I know her well. She was obviously affected by what happened to her, but I believed her. And what she told me makes me think that two people can sneak in where an army could not. We can save your friend."

The light from the moonglow amulet began to fan out ahead of Lithann as the tunnel widened suddenly.

"We've come to the end of the passage," she said, "but we have a problem."

Lithann peered into the opening as the light splayed out in all directions, including straight down. They'd come to the edge of a shaft that went straight down past the circle of her light.

*   *   *   *   *   *

"What's wrong?" asked Digur. He couldn't see very well past both the elf and her pet, even with the glow of Lithann's amulet illuminating the shaft in front of her.

"The tunnel just ends, and there's what seems to be a bottomless pit here," said Lithann. He could hear the frustration in her voice, but still wasn't sure what the problem was.

"I know," said Digur. He sat down, stretched his legs out, and began massaging his muscles. He was glad the narrow tunnel was high enough that he could sit. "We walled the rock devil access tunnel up all the way to the edge of shaft. We just have to climb down. It will take us all the way to their domain."

Lithann sighed. "I can't climb down a vertical shaft, and neither can Wiley," she said. She turned around with some difficulty to face Digur, her height making it hard to maneuver in the tight tunnel.

Digur furrowed his brows and asked, "Then how did you get down to our tunnels?"

"I summoned a gorilla and he carried us both down," replied Lithann. "But there's not near enough room here to summon such a huge beast." She stared hard at Digur, as if sizing him up for the first time. "Unless you can carry all of us down this shaft, I think we're stuck."

Digur mulled over the problem for a few minutes, all the while wondering how a race with such long arms and legs who lived their entire lives among the trees couldn't climb as well as a short, stocky dwarf. He assumed it must have something to do with motivation. Elves could always decide not to climb a tree, while dwarves lived under thousands of tons of rock and had to deal with the constant concern of the ground opening up beneath them.

Then he had an idea.

"Think we can all change places?" he asked. "I should be able to give you the room you need to summon your ape."

"Gorilla," said Lithann. She made a hand gesture to her pet, and it easily slipped past Digur as he slid to one side of the tunnel.

"Aren't they the same thing?" asked Digur as Lithann began crawling toward him. He flattened his back against the wall so she could crawl over his legs, but it was still a tight squeeze and the bow on her back smacked him on the side of the head as she went by.

"Close enough I guess," said Lithann, panting from exertion, but finally past him.

Digur crawled to the shaft and dangled his legs over the side. He could see fairly well even in the pitch black, but even he couldn't see the bottom of the pit. The height and darkness didn't bother him, though. What awaited them at the bottom, however, was another matter.

The dwarf gathered a small amount of mana in his hands and began to carefully craft a spell. He had to make some major modifications to it to make this work, but it wasn't much harder than spells he'd weaved during construction projects.

Mana poured from Digur's hands over the lip of the shaft and began to coalesce about a meter below his feet. He infused about half of the energy into the stone wall of the shaft, forcing it to seep into every crack and crevice, and follow every fissure and seam as far into the rock as he could drive it before it solidified.

The rest of the mana began building up on the surface of the wall, flowing outward into the open space of the shaft as well as around the perimeter. Layer after layer of mana built up and solidified into stone, forming a platform that extended out almost two meters into the pit.

As he finished the spell, Digur admired his handiwork. A horizontal wall of rock almost completely encircled the pit, almost seamlessly melding with the wall of the shaft, providing a safe and secure place to stand outside the tight tunnel.

Digur hopped down from the ledge and landed on the magical, stone platform. He peered over the edge and motioned to Lithann to join him before moving off to the side.

The elf came to the edge and peered over cautiously, her amulet illuminating the ledge and part of the shaft below. "Is it safe?" she asked. He could hear the worry in her voice and see the fear in her eyes.

Digur jumped up and down on his wall platform a few times, completely confident in his conjuration. "Safe as rock houses," he said. "Summon your big monkey and let's get to the bottom of this pit."

"Gorilla," said Lithann and laughed, but then her face scrunched up with concern again as she looked at the drop from the tunnel to the platform.

She turned around and dangled her feet over the edge, inching backward until she could feel the conjured rock wall under her toes. She then gingerly put her full weight on it, holding onto the ledge of the tunnel for a moment longer while she felt around with her feet.

The fox came to the edge next and dropped down onto the conjured ledge without a moment's hesitation. She sat at Lithann's feet and looked up at both of them, her tongue lolling out one side of her mouth.

Lithann walked around the rock platform, a bit gingerly at first, but then with increasing ease. "This is incredible," she said. "I never would have thought to use a horizontal wall as a platform."

Digur beamed with pride inside, a little taken aback by the compliment from someone who should be his sworn enemy.

Lithann stood in a pool of light, head bowed, as she began gathering mana to summon her gorilla. Seeing the light again, Digur remembered something he'd meant to say earlier. "You should darken your amulet when we start down."

Lithann finished casting her spell and the gorilla formed on the other side of the tunnel next to the open space where they would start their climb down. "Why?" she asked.

"The only way we will survive down in the rock devil tunnels is by not alerting them, any of them," said Digur. He pulled climbing tools out of his pack and then re-stowed his other gear.

"I have to be able to see," said Lithann. She had climbed onto the gorilla's back while the great ape leaned over to grab the fox in one huge, meaty paw.

"Find some way to dim it, at least," said Digur. "If even one rock devil sees us, they'll *all* know we're there. I don't know how they do it; they don't seem intelligent enough to have telepathy or spell casting, but they swarm as soon as even one is alerted."

"Hive mind," said Lithann matter-of-factly. "I think they're chimera—creatures created from the parts of many other creatures. I counted at least four, I think."

"How does that happen?" asked Digur as he moved around the platform to the edge opposite the gorilla. "It doesn't seem possible to meld that many together. And, the rock devils multiply faster than any other chimera I've ever heard about."

Lithann shrugged, "I don't know. I'm just telling you what I saw." She tucked her amulet under her leather armor, which dimmed the light extensively. "Better?"

"Much." Digur waited for his eyes to adjust to the darker conditions before moving.

The gorilla swung itself over the edge of the rock wall platform and began climbing down the wall, digging the claws from one huge paw and both feet into the stone for purchase. Digur attached spikes to his boots, donned a pair of spiked gloves, and followed.

They made good time climbing down the shaft. Digur was impressed with the gorilla's strength and climbing ability. As they neared the bottom of the pit, though, Digur thought he saw shapes moving in the darkness below the pale pool of light surrounding Lithann.

"Watch out," he hissed, but it was too late.

The gorilla must have sensed the floor of the pit was close because it jumped down the last five meters and landed in the middle of a pack of rock devils.

Digur climbed down the wall as fast as he could because he would be useless in this fight until he had his hands free.

Lithann yelped and dropped off the back of the gorilla as the rock devils came into the light. Her fox jumped right out of the gorilla's grip and attacked the closest beast, while the gorilla moved to block the advancing creatures from reaching the elf.

Unfortunately, Lithann didn't understand the rock devils as well as Digur. Two of the beasts simply ran up onto the wall of the shaft and skirted around behind the gorilla.

While the fox ripped out the throat of one rock devil, the gorilla crushed the head of another. Lithann focused on two more rock devils that clawed at the flanks of her creatures. She entangled one in vines and then pulled out her bow and pierced the other dead center in its chest.

The elf didn't seem to notice the two rock devils coming around behind her, though, and Digur wouldn't reach the floor of the shaft before they attacked. In a desperate move, he jumped free of the wall from over ten meters up, and gathered blue mana in his palms as he fell.

As he passed the rock devils crawling along the wall above Lithann, Digur spread his arms wide and unleashed waves of mana from his fingertips. The repulsion waves caught the rock devils and flung them off the wall and back down the tunnel, banging into one another along the way.

As Digur continued to fall, he tried to place a forcefield around his body, hoping it would protect him from breaking anything when he hit the floor. His spell was only half-cast, however, when his feet hit the stone floor.

Digur heard several sharp snaps as his ankles shattered. The sudden impact and the shooting pain searing through his legs broke Digur's concentration. The wisps of mana dissipated and slipped through his fingers as he crumpled to the floor and lost consciousness.

*   *   *   *   *   *

"Good," said Lithann. "You're awake."

She knelt beside Digur and placed her hands on his ankles. As she gently applied pressure to the joints, she studied his face. "Do you feel any discomfort?" she asked.

Digur shook his head and tried to speak. "No," he coughed out, his throat full of phlegm from lying on his back. He turned his head to the side and spat. By the light of her amulet, Lithann could see blood mingling with the spittle on the floor next to the dwarf. Her restorative magic hadn't healed all of his internal wounds yet.

"How long was I out?" he croaked.

"Several minutes," said Lithann. She probed his body a bit more, looking for tender areas. He grunted a bit when she reached his chest. "I think you have a couple of cracked ribs."

Digur pushed her hands away as she began channeling mana. "No time," he said. "We could be swarmed any second now."

Digur rolled to his side with a moan and pushed himself up to his feet. "Come on," he said. "We have to move." He stood there, unsteadily, for a moment before walking down the tunnel. Lithann noticed that the dwarf hunched forward as he walked, favoring the broken ribs.

She didn't argue, though. She just picked up her gear and followed, commanding Wiley and the gorilla to move ahead of Digur and take point.

"Lose the gorilla," said Digur with a grunt. "He won't fit."

"Fit where?" asked Lithann as she caught up to the dwarf. She offered her arm for him to lean on, but he waved it away.

"There's a small side-tunnel up ahead," said Digur pointing into the darkness beyond the small pool of light offered by Lithann's amulet. "We should be able to hide there and wait for the rock devil horde to pass us by…assuming we can reach it before they descend upon us."

"And if we don't make it in time?" asked Lithann.

"Then even your gorilla won't be able to save us," said Digur. "Dismiss it."

Lithann wasn't sure how she felt about taking orders from a dwarf, but Digur had risked his life to save her back at the shaft, so perhaps she ought to trust his guidance now. With a wave, she dismissed the gorilla, and then, as a sudden thought hit her, she unslung her bow and handed it to Digur.

"Lean on this," she said. "It will help ease the pain. Plus, if the entire rock devil tribe attacks us down here, I guess this won't help much either."

Digur smiled and grabbed the bow. Using it like a staff, he was able to straighten up a bit and walk a bit faster.

"It's not far," he said after a while. "Just around the next curve."

Lithann noticed the wall curving beside her in the dim light but couldn't see far enough ahead to know if the side tunnel had come into view yet. But at that moment, she knew it didn't matter. She heard the scrabbling sound of rock devils claws scraping against stone.

"Run!" screamed Lithann and Digur at the same time.

Lithann sprinted down the tunnel even though she was all but blind past the edge of her light, which barely illuminated a couple of meters around her.

The scrabbling sound ahead seemed to echo on forever, but Lithann began to realize she wasn't hearing echoes, but hundreds if not thousands of claws all scraping against rock all at once.

Lithann looked over to see how Digur was doing, but he wasn't there. She glanced over her shoulder, but couldn't see him behind her either.

"Digur!" she hissed as loud as she dared. "Are we almost there?"

"You are," he called back. "Keep going and you'll make it."

Lithann's mind jumped back to Digur's story about his previous flight from the horde of rock devils and his brother's sacrifice, and she slowed down.

"Go, go, go!" he yelled. "You can make it."

"No," she said as Digur hobbled up alongside her. "We both make it or…we don't. Either way, we do it together."

They jogged forward side by side, Digur grunting with every jarring step. Lithann pulled her amulet out from under her armor so she could see better. No sense hiding from the rock devils now.

She saw the tunnel. It was tantalizingly close. But she could also see the rock devil horde coming at them like a wall of water just beyond the opening. They covered every bit of the tunnel—floor, walls, and ceiling—like termites devouring the inside of a log.

The tunnel was too large to cover with a single wall spell and there was no way they could make it to the side tunnel before the rock devil wave swept over them. And yet, Digur soldiered on beside her.

He paused while running to cast a stone wall that blocked about half the tunnel. Thinking quickly, Lithann added a wall of thorns that extended from the top of the Digur's wall all the way up to the ceiling.

It wouldn't stop the horde, but it might slow them down enough for the two of them and Wiley to make it into the side tunnel.

"I only have one more rock wall," said Digur, huffing as he ran. "I have to save that to block the side tunnel behind us."

"Don't talk," said Lithann. "Run."

Digur screamed as he grabbed the bow under his armpit and began running in earnest. His broken ribs must have been tearing at his flesh and organs with every jarring step.

Lithann sent Wiley on into the tunnel ahead of them and began sprinting, but stayed behind Digur. She wanted to make sure he was inside the tunnel before he blocked it off. She wouldn't let him sacrifice himself for her.

A few rock devils forced their way through the brambles, bleeding from multiple scrapes and cuts suffered while pushing through the thorny vines.

The side tunnel loomed ahead of Lithann as a stream of bloody rock devils crawled down the tunnel wall toward them. She knew if they stopped to take care of the first wave, the rest of the horde would be on them before they could get to safety. There was nothing they could do now but run.

Lithann could tell they weren't going to make it. The first rock devil had reached the side tunnel. She thought about entangling it, but then heard a surprised yelp coming from Wiley inside the tunnel, and worried that their escape route was already overrun.

Then, a tall figure appeared in the entrance of the tunnel, arms raised, holding two glowing sticks. The figure raised one stick, and a blue beam leapt from it toward the first rock devil, which simply vanished.

The other stick then flashed and a bolt of lightning streaked from the tip toward the line of rock devils. The intense, white lightning blinded Lithann for a moment, but she kept running. As the spots in her eyes cleared, she could see that the lightning had fried all of the rock devils between her and the tunnel.

The tall figure stepped back as Digur ran inside the side tunnel. Lithann slipped inside just behind the dwarf, and took no more than three steps before the dwarf cast a wall of stone behind her. She collapsed on the ground, heaving and retching as she tried to catch her breath.

"We should leave here immediately," said a deep, elven voice from behind Lithann. "That wall will not hold the morga long. I know a safe place where you can rest."

CHAPTER 8: SAFE AND SOUNDS

Once Lithann could breathe again, she stood and turned toward their savior. He was tall for an elf—taller even than Jhonart—and stood with his back straight and his shoulders back, making him appear even taller, or perhaps just more regal. He was definitely not a wood elf.

He wore dark, purple robes lined in gold, and a long, blood-red stole embroidered with all manner of strange symbols and magical runes. He had such a severe, angular face that his cheeks and eyes looked sunken in the dim light. His straight, black hair was pulled back away from his forehead, which made his face look stretched and pulled tight.

He carried a black staff on his back that ended in a large, glowing ruby encircled by four floating stones. In his hands, he held two wands. One had a crystal shaft encircled by copper wire. Lithann could see blue energy swirling around inside the clear shaft. The other wand looked like a twisted piece of quicksilver. It seemed almost fluid as it curved and looped through itself from his hand to the tip. Flames licked at the silver wand along its entire length.

While this stranger looked impressive and he had certainly saved their lives, Lithann knew they couldn't move again until she tended to Digur's broken ribs, which had most likely sliced into some internal organs during their frantic dash for freedom. He wouldn't be able to walk far before falling unconscious again.

"Let me heal my friend first," she said to the strange elf, "and then you can lead us to your safe spot." Besides, she wasn't about to go anywhere with a stranger until Digur was in fighting shape again.

"No time," said the elf. "And no need." He sheathed his wands into a pair of long, thin leather pouches connected to his sash, and began channeling mana through his fingers.

"Wait a minute—" started Lithann.

Blue strands of mana snaked out from the elf mage's hands and began to envelop Digur.

"What are you doing?" yelled Lithann.

A moment later, Digur disappeared with an audible popping sound. It looked to Lithann like the mana-shrouded dwarf just folded in on himself.

"What did you do to Digur?" asked Lithann. She reached for her bow, but realized that Digur had still been holding it when he vanished.

"I sent the dwarf to my safe spot," said the elf. "Please pick up your fox and I will send the two of you there as well."

Lithann stared at the elf, considering her options. She might be able to defeat him alone, but she could already hear the rock devils or morga or whatever they were called clawing their way through the rock wall.

"Please, miss," said the elf. "We do not have much time. Your friend is fine. Otherwise his wall would have dissolved and we would both be dead."

Lithann couldn't argue with his logic, and her only chance to save Digur from internal bleeding lay through this elf's magics. She grabbed Wiley in a big hug and closed her eyes as the blue energy enveloped her.

She heard a loud pop that seemed to come from inside her brain and echo around inside her skull as a wave of nausea overcame her. She opened her eyes, feeling dizzy and needing to orient her body to help her stomach determine which direction was up again.

Digur lay in front of her in a pool of vomit. Lithann rushed to his side and almost vomited as well from vertigo. She was no longer in the tunnel. Instead, she found herself in a well-lit cavern bedecked with all the comforts of home.

A large mattress covered in silks sat in an alcove near the back. Across one wall sat several large chests that stood open showing clothes and gear and dry foodstuffs piled up inside. A gigantic wooden table strewn with papers, alchemical supplies, and a large, magical lantern dominated the middle of the cavern, while water poured out of a crack in the back wall like a fountain, streaming down into a perfectly circular shallow pool in the floor.

Lithann ignored her change in surroundings and concentrated on the dwarf in front of her instead. She cast several healing spells, directing their restorative power to Digur's ribs and internal organs, while trying to ignore the most disturbing part of the chamber the mage had sent them to.

It wasn't what she had seen in the cavern that worried Lithann the most.

It was what she didn't see. The chamber had no doors or doorways, no entrances or exits. They were completely shut in.

*   *   *   *   *   *

As Lithann worked to heal Digur, she heard another pop in the air behind her. Their host—or jailer—had joined them.

"How does your dwarven friend fare?" asked the tall elf as he came up behind Lithann.

She noticed that the mage made no sound as he walked across the stone floor. He was as stealthy down in the depths as she was in the forest.

She stood and turned toward the elf, keeping her body between him and Digur. "I've healed his wounds. Now he needs to rest to regain his strength."

The elf nodded, never moving his eyes away from her face as he stared for a moment longer. He then moved off toward the waterfall in the rear of the chamber, seemingly unconcerned with turning his back on Lithann.

She took a deep breath and tried to relax, but found her muscles were still tensed and ready for battle, so she forced a false calmness into her voice. "Thank you for your help," she said. "Digur and I would be dead if you hadn't been there."

"True," said the elf. He plunged his hands into the stream of water pouring out of the wall and splashed some on his face before turning around. "Are there any more of your group who need help?"

It was a simple question and the elf smiled as he spoke, but his eyes had a dark, penetrating quality, and his mouth twitched just slightly as he spoke, which made Lithann feel like she was talking to her old master, whose conversations were always a test, no matter how friendly they seemed.

"We've come looking for another…member of our group who was abducted by those—what did you call them? Morga?" she said, skirting his actual question. Lithann didn't want him to know that she and Digur were actually alone down here.

"Really?" he said, lifting one eyebrow. He didn't continue, although Lithann could tell that the abduction was news to him. Instead, he walked over to the table, sat down, and began writing on a piece of parchment.

Lithann stared at the odd elf for a moment and then glanced down at Digur, who seemed to be breathing easier, but remained unconscious. Seeing him asleep reminded her of how long it had been since she had slept. She placed his pack under his head and picked up her bow from beside the dwarf as casually as she could.

She motioned for Wiley to stay near the dwarf and then walked over to the table. "I am Lithann of the Straywood forest," she said. "And you are?"

"Forgive me," he said, looking up from his papers. "How rude of me. I am Inesta, Sortilege Wizard, at your service."

He bowed his head in a quick gesture of respect, but as with all of his movements, it seemed a bit too purposeful; not forced per se, but formalized and practiced, as if Inesta was acting a part.

"Sortilege," said Lithann. "I've heard of that. A conclave of Wizards, correct?"

"We are a small community of elves far to the southwest of here," said Inesta as he scribbled a few more notes, "on the coast of the Etherian Ocean. And yes, most of us are Wizards. We seek to learn all there is to know about this world."

Lithann glanced at the papers strewn across the table, and was amazed at the sheer number of pages of notes the Wizard had written. He'd covered the entire table with seemingly random piles of parchment, some of which had fallen over on other piles. The only bare space was the small section in front of the mage where he worked on the latest page.

"Is that why you are down here?" she asked. "Learning about these morga creatures?"

"That is correct," he said. "I have been tasked with studying the morga. They are fascinating creatures."

Lithann studied the top pages on several piles in front of her, but couldn't understand anything written on any of them. It was all in an obscure language—no, it was some highly intricate code using symbols that Lithann had never seen before along with letters and numbers.

"It would appear you have learned quite a lot," she said, trying to probe for more information—about the morga as well as about Inesta.

"Not as much as you would think," he said with a smile that Lithann thought looked a little forced. "These notes detail their lives, but much of it is repetitive—eat, sleep, reproduce, expand their habitat—all of which they are quite skilled at."

Lithann studied the desk while talking with Inesta, but even though the

Wizard used an intricate code system, it appeared he had absolutely no organizational system. Either that or the random piles strewn haphazardly across the desk were in fact set in some sort of highly evolved organizational system only Inesta understood. He probably knew where every piece of paper was stored in this mess.

"So an abduction of a wood elf from the surface is not normal then?" she asked as innocently as she could.

"No," said Inesta. "That is new, and more than a bit disturbing."

As Lithann studied the desk, she noticed a small section of a tunnel map peeking out from the edge of one of the piles. The rest of the map was almost completely obscured by the piles of parchments, although she could see bits of it here and there. It must have covered most of the table. However, the section she noticed contained a small chamber completely sealed off from the surrounding tunnels.

"Do you have any idea why they might have taken my...fellow elf?" she asked, forcing her eyes back to Inesta so he didn't notice what she was staring at.

Inesta took some time to answer. He was either considering her question or considering his answer. The Wizard was incredibly difficult to read and she was becoming increasingly tired, which made it all the more difficult to concentrate.

While he mulled over his answer, Lithann discreetly glanced at the bits of map she could see, looking for some clue about how to get out of this chamber or where the morga might have taken Jhonart.

"Possibly," said Inesta after a time. "And if I'm right, your friend may still be alive."

That caught Lithann's wandering attention. She stared at the Wizard. "Are you certain?" she asked.

"Nothing with the morga is ever certain," he replied. Inesta steepled his long fingers in front of his face and fell into deep thought.

Lithann waited for a long moment to see if the elf would continue. When he did not, she asked, "Well, do you know where they've taken him?"

Inesta looked at her over the tips of his fingers. "No," he said. Then he dropped his hands to his side and stood, as if he'd suddenly come to a decision. "But I know where they will take him next."

Upon hearing this news, Lithann felt a surge of adrenalin that made her momentarily forget about her fatigue. She moved toward Digur to wake him up. "Then take us there," she said over her shoulder. "We have to save him."

"I cannot," he said, but when Lithann turned and stared daggers at the Wizard, he quickly added, "Not yet. I must rest before I can teleport us back out of this chamber. We have time, of this I am certain."

He moved toward the bed, saying over his shoulder, "I would recommend that you rest as well. Retrieving your friend from the clutches of the morga will not be easy. It may, in fact, kill us all."

Lithann resigned herself to waiting, knowing he was right, even if he had some ulterior motives. She needed to rest. Her muscles ached from walking, crawling, and fighting all day. Plus her brain had almost completely turned to mush while talking with the Wizard. Conversation with Inesta was as much a battle as her duel with the Grax had been.

So, she lay down next to Wiley, using her pet's hindquarters as a pillow, knowing that Wiley would alert her if anyone or anything attacked her while she slept. The two of them had spent many a night curled up like this in the forest.

As Lithann dozed, her tired brain wandered through the day's events, putting things together in odd ways and making connections that her waking mind had not seen.

In the moment between semi-consciousness and full sleep, she abruptly sat up as a burning question leapt to the forefront of her brain. She looked at Inesta, but the elf was already asleep, his breathing even and loud.

"How did the Sortilege elves find out about the morga?" she wondered aloud to herself. "The dwarves only found out because they live down here and were attacked. And yet, Inesta has months and months of research notes, and Sortilege is hundreds of leagues away. How did they know?"

She filed that question away for later, doused her moonglow amulet, and let the darkness of unconsciousness envelop her.

* * * * * *

Digur awoke in the darkness in a strange place full of odd sounds and smells. The last thing he remembered was a strange mage, a bright light, a loud popping noise, and darkness. Oh, and pain: a lot of pain.

Now he lay in a dark chamber. The pain had disappeared, but his side was oddly warm, even though the rest of his body felt cold. The air smelled musty, like fur-lined boots that had been worn too many times mixed with a library filled with slightly damp scrolls.

And then there was an odd chorus of whispering, snoring, panting, and running water that melded together into a susurrus-like medley. It was this mélange of murmuring that had ultimately woken Digur.

The sounds had permeated his dreams. He had been dropped into the arena, which was slowly filling with water. Ripples ran across the surface, lapping against the sides of the arena, and making him choke and snort each time they rolled by. Above him, the viewing chambers were filled with rock devils, who all pointed at him and whispered. He heard them say, "Dwarf and elf, dwarf and elf, dwarf and elf" over and over again.

Now that he was awake, though, he still heard the same sounds. He mentally shook the cobwebs out of his brain and concentrated on each in turn. The panting, he realized quickly, came from Wiley. The fox lay between Digur and Lithann, who slept on her back, snoring, next to the fox.

He saw all of this easily, and not just due to his keen, dark, dwarven vision. A soft, bluish glow washed over the three of them from the other side of the chamber. The murmuring whispers also seemed to be coming from that direction.

Digur closed his eyes and turned his head slowly toward the source of the glow. He didn't speak or make any sudden movements because he thought it would be better if it appeared that he was still sleeping.

Keeping his eyes closed, Digur mentally tuned out the snoring and panting noises to his right, so he could focus on the whispering to his left. The odd water-gurgling sound made it hard to hear every word, though.

"No, the wood elf and dwarf are not alone," said the hushed voice. "There is at least one more elf and possibly more. That is what concerns me."

There was a long pause where the only sound Digur heard was running water. He opened one eye a slit and peered into the back of the chamber. A tall robed figure stood next to a tight, tubular waterfall and stared into the pool of water at its base. The light emanated from the water.

"Yes," whispered the figure. "It is containable, but first I must ascertain the scope of the breach."

The robed figure stopped speaking and cocked his head as if listening to far-off voices.

"Yes," he whispered. "It is troubling to see an elf and a dwarf this far deep and together. That is why I urge caution before containment."

The figure paused and listened again before continuing. "Yes, I agree.

Containment is the final solution. I simply request more time to study these new developments."

A short pause, followed by, "Thank you."

The figure waved his long robed arms over the pool of water, which went dark. Digur closed his eyes to let them adjust and to make sure his irises didn't glint off any other lights. He heard the figure cross the chamber and then heard a soft thump like something heavy falling onto a sack of straw.

Several minutes passed and then Digur heard the unmistakable sound of a second elf snoring in the chamber. The dwarf opened both eyes and turned on his side to look around. Although he saw everything like a dark silhouette against a black wall, he could make out the table in the middle of the room, the chests along one wall, and the bed with the snoring figure in the back.

Digur lay back down, but did not sleep. He kept his eyes wide open and thought about what he had heard while he idly scratched the fox between the ears.

CHAPTER 9: STORIES AND SUSPICIONS

Lithann awoke with paws digging into the small of her back, hot fox breath warming her neck, and the soothing sound of a waterfall nearby. It felt so normal that she forgot about the stress and pain of the last twenty-four hours. She rolled over to say good morning to Wiley and scratch her pet behind the ears, which had been their ritual for years. However, when Lithann opened her eyes, the reality of her current situation began to intrude on past memories of a normal life.

First, she couldn't see a thing. Not only was it dark, there simply was no light—no sun or moon, no stars or fireflies, no campfires, and no lanterns from distant villages—nothing but darkness.

Second, while she could hear Wiley panting next to her, and reach out to scratch the fox's ears—which got her a friendly lick in return—her keen elfin ears heard two other people breathing nearby. She always camped alone in the forest, and even when she did venture back to town, Lithann never had overnight company. She had no siblings and few friends, and the friends she did have were little more than acquaintances.

To be honest, other elves were put off by Lithann. They found her too outgoing, too gregarious. To be fair, though, Lithann found most other elves stuffy, stifling, and a bit boring.

Lastly, the ground, while cold like the forest floor, had a hardness and staleness to it that told her she was nowhere near dirt nor the plants and other living things that relied upon it to survive. She had slept on large rocks occasionally in the forest, especially to escape the moist ground of a riverbank, but even then she could smell the dirt and the plants.

There might be moss in this chamber, but this sterile cavern had never seen a flower, a berry vine, or a fruit tree. Lithann found she actually missed those things—missed her old life—even though she hadn't necessarily been happy in it.

She sat up and felt and heard Wiley stand, stretch, and then sit beside her.

"Bright morning," said a gruff voice beside her, startling Lithann a bit until she recognized the voice of Digur. "I think that's what you day folk say when you awake."

Lithann smiled in the dark. "It's 'good morning,'" she said. "Not that we have any idea if it's even morning."

"And you don't know if it's going to be good yet," said Digur. "But you do know it will be bright…above ground that is."

"Speaking of which," said Lithann. She commanded her moonglow amulet to shine beneath her leather jerkin, which filled their section of the cavern with a soft glow.

"Ooh!" grunted Digur. "Give a bit of warning before you do that." He shielded his eyes from the pale light with a forearm. "And I wish you had left it dark a bit," he continued, lowering his voice a bit. "We should talk about that *other* elf."

"His name is Inesta," said Lithann. She scooted closer to Digur so they could keep their voices low and turned her body to shield the light from the rear of the chamber. "He's a Wizard from the—"

"Sortilege," said Digur. "I know. I recognized the robes and the haughty—haughtier than wood elf—demeanor."

"Oh, did you talk with him while I slept?" asked Lithann.

"Not exactly," said Digur. He leaned in closer and spoke so softly Lithann wasn't sure she caught every word. "I don't know what he told you, but that elf is not what he seems. I heard him talking to the waterfall."

Lithann raised an eyebrow and cocked her head. "To the waterfall?" she said. "Did it talk back to him?"

"No," said Digur in a dramatic whisper. "No, no no! I'm serious. I think he was communicating through a portal."

Lithann mulled this over a bit. She had never heard of a spell that could allow a mage to speak with someone over long distances, but her knowledge was limited to wood-elven magic. She had never heard of anyone in the Straywood sending messages this way, but it could be possible. If Inesta could teleport, why not speak through a portal?

"Okay," she said. "I get it. What did he say?"

"What did who say?"

Lithann and Digur both looked up to see Inesta standing over them, looking ghastly pale in the soft glow from the amulet. A shudder ran down Lithann's back as his gaunt face stared down at them, his eyes completely lost in shadow, looking like the dark sockets of a skeleton.

Digur stood and faced Inesta, barely coming up to the belt tied around the Wizard's robe. The size difference didn't deter Digur from confronting the much taller elf.

"I heard you talking to someone through that pool over there last night about your 'final solution,'" said Digur.

"Yes?" said Inesta. "And?"

Lithann stood and pulled her amulet out from beneath her armor because the skeletal Inesta was starting to freak her out.

"You mean to kill us, don't you," said Digur.

The thought had crossed Lithann's mind, but she was surprised to hear Digur state it so matter-of-factly.

"If I had wanted you dead," said Inesta, "we wouldn't be having this conversation. I simply could have allowed the morga to reach you in the tunnels."

Lithann nodded her head. "He did save us out there, Digur. And neither of us was in any shape to fight him off while we slept."

Digur appeared to think it over for a bit, before replying. "Then what was all that about containment and final solutions?" he asked.

Inesta smiled at them both and laughed a sharp, short laugh. "As I told your elf friend here, I was sent here to study the morga, but there is more to it than that."

"What do you mean?" asked Digur.

Inesta moved toward the table and motioned for them to follow. "Come, let me show you."

He picked up a pile of papers and almost immediately pulled a section of pages out of the middle, which he spread out across the table. Several showed drawings of the morga with lines connecting various body parts to images of animals—ants to the mandibles, badgers to the claws, etc. The drawing showed that more than a dozen species had been combined to create the morga. The most disturbing was rodents, which seemed to be connected to the morga's reproductive system.

Inesta pointed to another set of pages that held a table of data. Lithann couldn't read the codes, and her quizzical look must have prompted Inesta to explain. "These rows list termination methods, such as poisons, gasses, environmental catastrophes, elemental forces, magical spells, etc.," he said, pointing at the table. "The columns show efficiency data for each method. Sadly, none are terribly efficient."

He dropped the pages back onto the table. "The morga are a threat to every race in the world," he said. "So, we of the Sortilege are looking for a way to exterminate them. If left unchecked, they will literally consume everything and everyone. We are determined to not allow that eventuality to come to pass."

"So 'containment' is…" said Digur, trailing off.

"A euphemism," finished Inesta, "for genocide, yes."

Lithann gasped. "That's monstrous," she said. "Even for something as monstrous as these creatures."

Inesta shook his head. "Look, the morga are not natural creatures," he explained, pointing at the drawings. "They were created not by gods but by mortals; and mortals make mistakes. The morga were a mistake, a horrible mistake that will destroy the world. The Sortilege has a reputation for being willing to make hard choices, so we have made this choice, and we have made it for the sake of all races."

"How do you know so much about the morga?" asked Digur. His tone of voice did not hide his obvious distrust of Inesta.

"Why because we created them, of course," said Inesta.

"You created them?" asked Lithann. A rush of emotions churned inside her as she thought about everything that had happened to Jhonart, Artemis, and Digur's brother.

As the thought of Dargur, Lithann covered her gaping mouth with her hand and turned to face Digur. He'd balled his fists and stared hard at the Wizard, as if willing him to die with his eyes.

"Not me, personally," said Inesta. "A misguided mage who thought he could play at being a god. He was punished and we, the rest of the conclave, are working to correct his mistake."

"Doesn't matter who amongst you did it," said Digur. "You all will pay the price for the death of my brother, and I might as well start with you."

Digur brandished his force blade and turned to move around the table. Lithann grabbed him by the shoulder. "We need him, Digur," she said. "He knows where the morga have taken Jhonart. Besides, if you kill him, we'll be stuck in this chamber forever."

"I can dig us out of here," said Digur through clenched teeth, "after I gut this heartless bastard."

Inesta held his hands up in front of him, palms forward, in the universal sign of surrender. "We can settle this debt after I help this young elf rescue her friend," he said. "I give you my word."

"What good is that?" asked Digur. "What good is the word of a member of a race that would create monstrous eating machines and unleash them on an unsuspecting world without a word of warning? You die now."

"Digur, please!" cried Lithann. She held the dwarf by both shoulders and looked deep into his eyes. A tear rolled down her cheek. "Please think about Jhonart. We need Inesta. I...I need him to save my friend, my...my brother. Please. Settle this later."

Even though Jhonart wasn't really Lithann's brother, Digur's eyes softened and his shoulders slumped when she used the fraternal term. "Okay," he said. "I'll put this aside for now, for you and for Jhonart."

The dwarf dimmed his force blade and returned it to its sheath and then turned to stare at Inesta. "But when this is over, you and I are going to dance."

Inesta smiled and dropped his hands to his sides. "I knew there was a reason I saved your life," he said. "I haven't had this much fun in months!"

Convinced that the danger of a mage duel breaking out in the tiny chamber had passed, Lithann turned to Inesta and asked: "When do we leave to search for Jhonart?"

"Soon," said Inesta. "First we must find a way for Lithann to traverse the morga tunnels without shining like a beacon." He pointed at her glowing amulet.

"Jhonart tried to teach me how to see through my pet's eyes," she replied, "but I never quite got the knack of it. I always ended up falling over or feeling like my head was going to split open."

"It is a tough trick," said Digur, "but all you really need is practice."

"No time like the present to perfect the technique," said Inesta.

"Just take it easy at first and stick close to your pet," said Digur.

Lithann called Wiley over and commanded the fox to stand beside her. She then extended her consciousness into her pet's mind and accessed Wiley's senses. She saw the room overlapping at two different heights in her brain. She tried to walk around, but the double vision made her feel nauseous within just a few seconds.

She stopped and took a few deep breaths until the bile welling up in her throat began to subside. "It's no good," she said. "The double vision always gets to me."

Digur snapped his fingers. "Douse your light, elf," he said. "In the dark, you'll only have the wolf's sight and not your own."

"Fox," said Lithann almost automatically. But then she snapped her fingers as well. "Great idea. I never thought of that. I'm as blind as tree down here without my amulet, which will actually be an advantage."

She commanded the amulet to darken and tried again. While she bumped into things at first as she walked around the chamber, and almost fell into the waterfall pool at one point, she no longer had any double vision problems.

"It works," she said after a few minutes.

"Excellent," said Inesta. "I will prepare for our departure. I suggest you keep practicing until we are ready to go."

*　　*　　*　　*　　*　　*

Digur repacked his gear while simultaneously keeping an eye on Lithann's progress and Inesta's preparations. He wanted to make sure that his ally didn't hurt herself and that his enemy didn't hurt either of them.

He didn't care what excuses the Wizard gave them for his conversation during the night, Digur knew what he had heard and knew who the final solution would be directed against. Years of dealing with Minister Grimhammer had taught Digur one thing: people in power will do everything they can to remain in power, including hiding the truth and removing anyone who uncovers their lies.

A short time later, Inesta had finished rooting through his own gear and returned to the table. "I am nearly ready," he said. "I will teleport us all to an observation post I established near the morga nest."

Digur did not love the idea of letting the Wizard teleport them into the unknown, but nodded his head anyway. He just kept reminding himself that Inesta could have killed them any number of times already. He was obviously waiting for something; Digur simply had to guess what it was and be ready to act when the time came.

Inesta pulled out the crystal wand he had used to make the morga disappear in the side tunnel the day before and began infusing it with a spell.

"There," he said. "I never required more than a couple of teleport spells in a day before, but I suspect we'll need a plethora today. Who will go first?"

Digur spoke up before Lithann could answer. "Send Lithann first," he said.

"Fine," said Inesta. "Grab your fox just like before and I can send you both."

Digur watched as Lithann and the fox folded in on themselves and disappeared with a pop. He hoped he would see the two of them on the other side. He'd grown quite accustomed to their company. A moment later, Digur felt his body being pulled into a collapsing, dark portal. It felt so like being drunk—and not the pleasant kind of drunk he reached after imbibing great quantities of alcohol, but how the liquid feels when being gulped down a thirsty throat.

The first thing Digur noticed on the other side was that Inesta had been true to his word. He had teleported them to a little chamber with a number of small slits carved into the wall. He stood on his tiptoes and stretched to look looked through one of them. He could see a large chamber on the side with a dozen tunnels leading off in all directions.

Digur heard a popping sound behind him and turned to see Inesta arrive out of nothingness in the back of the small chamber.

"Excellent," said Inesta. "Any activity present?" he asked as he moved to the view port next to Digur. He looked through the slit without even waiting for an answer.

"As I suspected," he said. "Completely empty. Excellent. It is time."

Digur's hand went immediately to his force blade. "Time for what?" he asked.

"No time to explain," he said. "We must hurry or your friend will not survive long enough to be rescued."

Lithann gasped beside Digur, so he didn't press the Wizard to explain himself. "Then what are we waiting for, Wizard?" he asked.

Inesta waved his crystal wand again and pointed it at Digur. "Wait for me down there in the chamber," he said as he teleported the dwarf again.

A few moments later, their little group stood in the middle of the huge morga chamber and the queasiness Digur felt from having his body sucked down a dimensional drain twice in a matter of minutes had subsided enough for him to follow Inesta toward one of the tunnels at a brisk jog.

"This way," said the Wizard. "Quickly."

As he ran, Digur stared at the walls of the chamber and tunnels. In all of his previous trips, he had been running for his life and had not had the time to really study the morga's handiwork. Every surface was covered in grooves, yet the floor was remarkably flat and level and the walls rose up to an almost perfect dome. Morga digging skill nearly matched his own.

"Where are we going?" asked Lithann a bit breathlessly. She was obviously having trouble keeping up while concentrating on seeing in the inky blackness through her pet's eyes.

Digur forgot his fascination with the tunnel walls and jogged up beside the wood elf to be ready to catch her should she stumble.

"The morga are inquisitive creatures," said Inesta as he loped down the tunnel on his long legs. "They are studying us as much as we study them. I don't know why yet, but they have begun emulating some of the traits of the higher races."

He stopped briefly at an intersection to check the cross tunnels, and then turned left and continued on. Digur noted the direction change in case they had to retreat without the Wizard.

"What do you mean, 'emulating us'?" asked Lithann. She gasped for air while Inesta answered, and Digur began to wonder if Inesta's pace had more to do with hampering Lithann's fighting prowess than a sense of urgency over her friend's fate.

"They have a hive mind," said Inesta, "so they really have no need to congregate. What one morga sees or hears or experiences, all others will experience. But lately, they have begun to gather together at specific time intervals for special events that all can experience at the same time."

The group slowed down at another intersection and, after checking for morga activity down the other tunnels, the Wizard turned right. This back and forth happened several more times before they reached their final destination.

"And these events emulate something other races do?" asked Digur as he took note of the latest change in direction.

"Exactly," said Inesta. He slowed down to a walking pace as they approached an opening, eventually coming to a stop.

"What kind of event?" asked Lithann as she doubled over behind the Wizard and gulped air into her lungs.

Digur came up beside Inesta and felt his jaw go slack as he gazed into the chamber beyond the opening. It was an enormous arena, easily five times larger than the Anvil Throne arena. Thousands of morga packed multiple levels of viewing chambers above an expansive arena floor that dwarfed a single male wood elf standing alone in the center, like a solitary tree jutting up from the side of a mountain after an avalanche had leveled everything else in its devastating path.

"Arena combat," said Inesta.

CHAPTER 10: MORGA ARENA

Jhonart stood in the middle of a large, black emptiness. He felt the vastness of the chamber open up around him as soon as the beasts carried him through the doorway. They dumped him on the cold stone floor and scattered out of sight, climbing up distant walls, if the sound of their scrabbling claws was any indication.

His entire body ached. He'd saved himself the full brunt of the fall into the pit by casting a quick conjuration that gave his body a kinship to the body of the bear he'd summoned, toughening his skin to absorb some of the impact.

Even so, Jhonart knew he'd broken several ribs and suffered a concussion when he hit the bottom of the pit, and the fall had knocked him out cold. He'd awoken curled up in a small chamber. When he'd tried to stand, he found the stone room was barely a meter and a half high and not much longer, so he ended up sitting hunched over or lying in a ball for hours.

Every muscle in his body screamed at him as he stretched them back out now that he could stand. He'd been able to cast a couple of minor healing spells while crammed into the stone cell, but he still felt stabbing pains radiating across his chest with every breath, and his head felt like it had grown twice as large over night.

Just as Jhonart began to think about making a run for it, strange noises began emanating somewhere in the distance above him. It sounded like apes grunting or whooping, a sound he had heard before. But there was something different about these sounds. Each grunt or whoop began and ended with a sharp click that echoed around the huge chamber. The sound sent a shiver down the elf's spine as it grew in volume and spread around him, eventually becoming a deafening roar of grunts, whoops, and clicks from every direction.

Jhonart could see a small area directly around him through the eyes of a ferret he'd summoned while stuck in the cell. He'd tucked the narrow-bodied rodent underneath his bearskin jerkin and it stuck its head up under his chin when he needed to see.

The ferret could only see in black-and-white, though, and the total lack of light limited even its eyesight quite a bit. So, Jhonart could only see about twenty meters and viewed everything as shadows moving through deeper shadows.

Several shadow creatures detached themselves from the darkness at the edge of his sight and moved toward Jhonart. Their hunched gait told him the three creatures in front of him were the same unholy monsters who had taken him prisoner. The scrabbling noises the elf heard at his back told him three more were moving in from behind.

Jhonart gathered most of his mana reserves and summoned another steelclaw grizzly. He also released the ferret from his armor so it could aid in the coming battle.

Jhonart had spent some time dueling in the Straywood arena, and in fact had won more than his fair share of combats there, so he knew how to survive tough battles. What he didn't know was why these subterranean monsters wanted to fight him in their underground arena, or what their rules might be—or even if there were any rules at all!

The order of the moment was survival, and that meant he needed allies. He already had two creatures, and his ferret was no ordinary rodent, but the legendary Sosruko. Jhonart knew the ferret wouldn't last long against a mob of these monsters—and he needed the ferret's eyes to see—so the Beastmaster quickly cast rhino hide to protect his companion and regrowth to allow the ferret to heal minor wounds on its own.

By the time Jhonart finished casting the second enchantment on the ferret, the monsters were on them. Sosruko intercepted the first attacker, deftly avoiding its claws by twisting its lithe body in a circle around the creature's limbs and then ran up the beast's arm and nipped at its neck, drawing a thin stream of blood.

As the ferret attacked the monster in front of Jhonart, the Beastmaster caught glimpses of the battle behind him through its eyes. The grizzly roared and slashed at the first monster with its giant paw, slicing the attacker in half from left shoulder down to its right hip. Upon seeing their companion cut in twain, the other two changed direction and dashed to either side of the bear to avoid its massive claws.

At that moment, the other two beasts in front of Jhonart attacked. The claws of the first scratched across his armor. He could feel the force of the attack down in his ribs, but it did no lasting damage. The second clawed at his exposed thigh below his armor and cut into his aching muscle.

Jhonart screamed in pain from the cut.

*   *   *   *   *   *

After the long run through the tunnels, Lithann bent over at the waist, placed her hands on her knees, and gulped huge mouthfuls of air into her lungs. Wiley turned toward her master and licked the elf's face, perhaps worried that Lithann was injured in some way.

She heard Digur and Inesta talking, and even participated in the conversation, but her mind had gone foggy with exertion, so the meaning of their words didn't register right away. Plus, with Wiley licking her face, Lithann was all but blind. All she could see was her own cheeks and nose and mouth, looking huge and out of focus.

When she heard the grunts, clicks, and whoops of the morga echoing back and forth across a giant chamber ahead of her, the word 'arena' finally struck a chord deep down in Lithann's brain. She forgot all about catching her breath and commanded Wiley to turn around. After taking one last deep breath to calm her body and mind, Lithann sent her senses back into her pet's brain.

Lithann looked into the huge chamber through Wiley's eyes, but couldn't see far enough through the pitch black to know what was happening. But, when she heard Jhonart scream, her worst fears were realized. She tried to rush into the arena to stand beside her friend, but Inesta stepped in her way and grabbed her by the shoulders.

"We cannot intercede," said Inesta, staring hard at her. "Not for the moment in any respect."

"Why not?" asked Lithann.

Beside her she heard Digur grunt in response to her question. "Yeah," he said. "Why the dirt not?"

Inesta softened his stare and loosened his grip on Lithann. "I have seen many of these duels," he said. "It will start gradually, with the morga sending a handful of attackers at a time to test the abilities and resolve of the prisoner."

"Which would seem the ideal time to intercede," said Digur gruffly. "Let's pull the elf out of there before the place gets too thick with dirt devils."

"If we do that now," said Inesta, "the stands will empty and we'll have to fight our way through every morga in the hive to get back into this tunnel."

"Won't that happen anyway?" asked Lithann. "Swarming seems to be what these monsters do best."

"Not if we time it right," said Inesta. "The morga won't allow us to spoil their event by turning the tide immediately, and they will retaliate with lethal numbers. However, if we insert ourselves into the middle of the battle and heighten the excitement, they will only respond with proportional numbers to maintain the advantage and prolong the event as long as possible."

"So, we have to wait until Jhonart is losing badly before we can save him?" asked Lithann. "That's insane. I can't even see what's happening out there."

"Trust me to know the right moment," said Inesta. He smiled at Lithann, but it did nothing to warm her heart or calm her nerves.

"Trust me to not let your brother die," said Digur. "I do think the Wizard is right. We need to do this carefully to prevent the bulk of the morga from spilling out of those stands. There must be thousands of them."

Digur furrowed his brows and scratched at his beard a moment. "I just wish there was some way to get a message to your friend so he could start moving toward us. That would make this a lot easier."

"I have an idea," said Lithann.

*　*　*　*　*　*

Jhonart had withstood the initial onslaught. The ferret eventually sliced open the neck of the beast it had attacked, leaving it laying in a pool of its own blood. The grizzly chased down one of the runners and sliced open the beast's torso with a quick slash of claws and then turned its attention to one of the creatures attacking the Beastmaster.

For his part, Jhonart bashed the beast clawing at his leg over the head with his staff, cracking its skull and knocking it unconscious and then gathered enough mana to summon another creature to help him stem the tide; this time he chose a timber wolf. Its thick hide would help protect it, so he wouldn't have to waste more mana on an enchantment, and it could deal decent damage with its claws.

The wolf and the ferret finished off the third monster in front of Jhonart, while he and the grizzly teamed up against the last runner, which had tried to flank the elf after fleeing the grizzly.

His early success in the fight, and the surge of adrenalin a battle always gave him, made Jhonart feel much better. His muscles had loosened up and his mind felt as sharp as a rose thorn. After he and the grizzly dispatched the final monster of what he assumed was just the first wave of many, he cast a minor healing spell to close up the wound on his thigh and began thinking about how to get out of this mess.

The problem was that he was blind past twenty meters, so had no idea which way to run to find a way out or if the arena even had any exits other than the one that led back to his cell. He could simply move toward a wall, but then his attackers could drop on him without warning.

At least out in the middle, he'd have a chance to react when the next wave arrived, which happened sooner than he expected. Through the ferret's eyes, he saw at least six of the monstrous beasts charging at him from one direction. He commanded the ferret to turn around and saw another six beasts loping across the stone floor on all four limbs from behind.

Jhonart commanded both the ferret and the wolf to face different directions. He switched his senses back and forth between the two animals to keep an eye on the entire battle, while setting the grizzly loose to do what it does best: tear the nasty beasts apart.

Sosruko took a ferocious hit from the first attacker that would have turned a lesser ferret into a bloody mess, but the rodent's enchanted hide came to its rescue, and it somehow held onto its attacker and sunk its teeth deep into the beast's forearm.

The second monster to reach Jhonart met the wolf instead. It tried to claw out the canine's eyes, but the wolf ducked under the blow and the attacker's claws caught in the animal's thick coat. The wolf pressed its advantage, lifting its head up inside the monster's reach and clamping its massive jaws down on the creature's neck. Jhonart heard its spine snap under the pressure.

Jhonart heard the grizzly engage in a ferocious battle with several other monsters off to his left, but had no time to switch his senses to the ursine as four more monsters were almost on him.

He entangled one and smashed another in the face with his staff, but two more had flanked the elf. One came at him from the left, and Jhonart was able to parry the creature's attack with his staff, but when he turned to check on the other attacker, the elf saw it leaping at him, its claws extended and ready to rake him across the face or slice open his jugular. Jhonart had no time to react.

At the last second, the leaping attacker went flying sideways as a red-and-black blur of fur carried it to the ground. Standing astride the downed monster, the Bitterwood fox's head snapped down and ripped out the throat of her opponent with a mighty chomp.

"Wiley!" said Jhonart, dumbfounded. "What are you doing here?"

Lithann's pet smiled a bloody smile at Jhonart and wagged her tail before running off toward the grizzly.

*   *   *   *   *   *

"You should not have done that," said Inesta.

Lithann heard the Wizard's boots shuffle on the stone floor and his voice got a little louder. He must have turned away from the arena to scold Lithann. She couldn't see him with Wiley off helping Jhonart.

"You could have alerted them to our presence here," continued the elf Wizard.

Lithann watched as Wiley pulled a morga off the grizzly's back and bit clean through its leg. "That's why I had Wiley loop halfway around the arena before heading into the center," she said. "Besides, they're fighting a Beast-master. The morga won't take notice of one more animal."

"And now you can lead your friend back here toward us," said Digur. "Good thinking."

Lithann smiled, both at Digur's compliment and at the deaths of two more morga out in the arena. "Exactly," she said, "as soon as there's a clear path for him, which should be quite soon."

"I don't recommend this path," said Inesta, "but if you insist on guiding your friend and the morga to our present location, please do so gradually so as to not arouse their suspicion. The morga are much more intelligent than most people give them credit."

"You sound like you admire the bloodthirsty monsters," said Digur. The scowl on his face was as evident in his words as if Lithann had seen it herself.

"I simply do not underestimate them," said Inesta, "which is how I have survived down here so long."

"Be quiet both of you," said Lithann. "This is my chance."

*   *   *   *   *   *

Jhonart found himself and his animals had come through the second wave of monsters practically unscathed. Sosruko's regrowth enchantment had closed the minor wound he had suffered and the wolf only had a minor scratch across its snout, which if anything had just made it fight more fiercely.

During the wave, Jhonart had even found enough time to summon an emerald tegu lizard and imbue it with the speed of a cheetah, thinking he might be able to ride the reptile out of the arena if he got the chance.

Wiley came padding over to Jhonart, her long snout smeared with the blood of the monsters; and yet, the fox looked like she was smiling as her tongue lolled over sharp teeth out one side of her mouth.

Lithann's pet looked him in the eye and he almost felt like there was more than animal intelligence staring up at him. She then grabbed his hand in her mouth, gently pressing her teeth against his skin to gain a firm hold.

"Stop!" commanded Jhonart as he tried to shake his hand loose.

The fox growled and pressed down on his hand harder with her teeth, drawing several pricks of blood from his palm. She then began sidestepping around the Beastmaster, still holding on firmly.

Jhonart had little choice but to turn his body or risk those pinpricks becoming long rips in his skin. But he knew more monsters would soon be upon them. He could already hear them scrabbling down the walls, and this time it sounded like an army.

Wiley finally stopped turning and began backing up, pulling Jhonart away from the center of the arena by his hand. He resisted at first, but then finally realized what the fox was doing. "Is Lithann over there?" he asked.

The fox released his hand and nodded, which was perhaps the oddest thing Jhonart had ever seen. In that moment, Wiley reminded him a lot of Lithann. He'd never subscribed to the adage that Beastmasters tended to look just like their animals, although he had to admit that he'd chosen Artemis because of the falcon's regal demeanor.

"Enough musing," said Jhonart to himself. He commanded his animals to follow, and began moving slowly in the direction Wiley had indicated. He didn't want to simply run for it yet because he had no idea how many of the monsters might appear between him and freedom, and he didn't want to outrun his sight range.

A moment later, Jhonart thanked the sun and stars for his intelligence and insight. Ahead of him, he saw a dozen of the burrowing creatures clambering out of a three-meter-wide, fifteen-meter long channel that curved around him. Had he been running, Jhonart would have assuredly fallen in.

As it was, he couldn't move forward any farther. The dozen diggers climbed out of their impromptu moat and stood behind it. They clicked their claws together and whooped, staring at something behind the elf.

Jhonart turned and saw at least two dozen more shadowy beasts moving toward him.

He was trapped!

CHAPTER 11: PITS AND PLANS

"Jhonart's in trouble!" screamed Lithann. "We have to go now!"

She rushed past Digur, who made no attempt to stop her, and somehow slipped past Inesta, who reacted too slowly to stop the elf even though she couldn't see him.

Digur did not immediately move to follow Lithann, instead keeping an eye on the Wizard to see how he would react.

"Her rash actions will be the downfall of us all," said Inesta. "Follow her at your own peril."

"I plan too," said Digur as he watched Inesta carefully, glancing into the arena to make sure his ally had not found immediate trouble.

As soon as Digur saw the Wizard raise his crystal wand, the dwarf put his plan into action. He'd assumed Inesta would leave them to die in the arena and was ready for him.

Before the Sortilege elf could cast the teleport spell he'd imbued into the wand, Digur raised one hand and unleashed the spell he'd prepared for this moment. A tendril of energy whipped out toward Inesta from the mana surrounding Digur's hand and enveloped the wand.

With a quick flick of his wrist, the dwarf snapped the line of energy like a rope, yanking the wand from the Wizard's hand and sending it flying end over end into the Forcemaster's other hand.

"What are you doing?" screamed Inesta, his eyes wide in horror and his fingers flexing at his sides as if he wanted to strangle Digur.

The look on Inesta's face was worth all the pain and anguish Digur had suffered since his humiliation in the arena against the Grax. But he wasn't done yet.

"Making sure you're with us until the end," replied Digur as he cast the second spell he'd readied.

Digur thrust both mana-infused hands forward, propelling a thick, sinewy column of bluish-white energy straight at Inesta's chest. As the energy reached the Wizard, the end of the column spread into smaller wisps that formed a skeletal hand. The hand slammed into Inesta and pushed him through the doorway into the arena.

Digur smiled at the Wizard as he skidded to a halt next to Lithann. "You'll get this back when we all leave the arena," said the dwarf as he pocketed the wand.

Inesta glared at Digur and opened his mouth, apparently to hurl some elfish epithet at the dwarf, but at that moment another half-dozen morga dropped off the wall between him and the dwarf.

Digur hadn't seen that coming, but for once, seeing a pack of ravenous morga a few meters away didn't scare him at all. It merely strengthened his resolve. He strode into the arena calmly planning his next move.

*   *   *   *   *   *

As Lithann sprinted into the arena, she experienced a moment of vertigo as she saw herself—through Wiley's eyes—appearing out of the darkness and running full speed toward the pit from behind the line of morga.

She came to a sudden stop before running into the back of the monsters. "Jhonart!" she yelled. "Eyes closed!" She then clamped her own eyelids closed and watched for the monster's reaction through Wiley's senses.

As expected, the morga between Lithann and the pit turned and began to advance. She reached into her armor, pulled out the moonglow amulet, and commanded it to shine.

The morga nearest her screamed and clamped their clawed paws over their faces to shield their eyes. Lithann opened her own eyes as she let the amulet dangle on its silver chain on her chest, and reached for her bow.

Before the beasts could see her clearly, Lithann had dropped three of them with clean shots through their throats, clearing a path between her and the pit.

"Digur!" she yelled over her shoulder. "We need a wall bridge over that pit!"

When the dwarf didn't answer immediately, Lithann turned around just in time to see Inesta almost slide into her as if pushed from behind and six morga drop off the wall between them and Digur.

*　　*　　*　　*　　*　　*

Jhonart opened his eyes after the bright initial flash of light from Lithann's amulet. It felt good to be able to see again and, he had to admit, it warmed his heart to see Lithann's face in the distance.

However, as Lithann pulled out her bow, Jhonart knew he had work to do just to get to the pit. He commanded his animals to guard him and quickly summoned a bobcat to swell the ranks of his animal allies.

Jhonart needed time to put the plan that was forming in his mind into action, and knew he would have to take a few hits before everything came together. So, he cast the same spell he'd used to toughen his body when he fell into the pit, giving him kinship with all his animals.

Several of the monstrous beasts attacked as Jhonart began inching his way back toward the pit. His animal companions intercepted the first three, taking some minor damage, even through their magical and non-magical protections.

Sosruko evaded his attacker and then bit right through its tendon. The wolf suffered another set of claws to the snout, which trailed across its eye, leaving a nasty, oozing wound. But that monster paid for the pain it caused by losing half its face in a mighty chomp.

Several of the beasts tried to take down the grizzly, clawing at its thighs and torso. Blood matted its fur, but didn't slow the bear down. It grabbed one of the monsters and ripped it in two.

Jhonart looked to Wiley, worried about his friend's pet, but the fox had disappeared. He could hear its claws clicking against the stone behind him.

As Jhonart and his animals inched their way toward the pit, more beasts poured out of the galleries and joined the mob moving toward him. The Beastmaster couldn't worry about that, though. He simply needed to stay alive until he reached the pit, which would funnel all the monsters into a nice, tight group.

He healed the grizzly and the wolf as he moved, while they guarded him from the encroaching horde. Jhonart checked his progress periodically, not by turning his head, which he knew would invite the creatures to attack, but by switching his senses back into Sosruko.

The ferret scanned the area behind Jhonart shortly after gnawing off the leg of its current attacker. He still had a ways to go before reaching the pit, and the wounds on his animals were piling up. The bobcat had already been taken down, while the fur on the grizzly's torso and legs was thick with blood and completely matted against its body.

Jhonart inched back ever more, while casting extra enchantments on his beasts. He needed to save some of his healing spells for himself and Lithann should they get themselves out of this mess.

He made the lizard as savage as a lion, and watched it charge down one of the monsters and remove its head in a single bite. Jhonart then used his last regrowth enchantment on the grizzly in the hopes that it might heal itself enough to stay alive.

Jhonart then checked his progress through Sosruko's eyes once again and saw that he was getting close. However, he also caught sight of another set of monsters dropping off the wall behind Lithann and the Wizard. He also saw a dwarf casting spells behind the newest horde of monsters, back near a tunnel leading off from the arena. He had no idea if the dwarf was friend or foe.

"Is the Anvil Throne behind this attack?" asked Jhonart under his breath. "If so, none of this may even matter."

Jhonart knew he couldn't wait any longer, though. It was time to act. He channeled misty mana into both palms and raised his arms up in front of him. In a second, the mist enveloped his arms and began snaking its way out toward his enemies.

Jhonart flung his arms forward and the ball of foggy mana split into at least two score of misty tendrils that shot out and enveloped the heads of all the monsters caught inside the arcing pit. A moment later, every member of the mob that had trapped Jhonart fell into a deep sleep and dropped to the stone floor. He'd used their own trap against the beasts.

He turned around and began looking for a way to get over the pit, but the area was enveloped in a roiling cloud of green gas. Jhonart considered jumping through the gas and trying to make it across the pit, but at that moment, the cloud dissipated and Jhonart saw a stone bridge. However, Lithann was in real trouble on the bridge.

*　　*　　*　　*　　*　　*

A plan began to form in Digur's head as soon as Lithann called for him to make a bridge over the pit. First, though, he needed to reach her side. Unfortunately, at least a dozen morga now stood between them and, as far as Digur could tell, Inesta had done nothing but encircle his body with lightning since being pushed into the arena.

"Inesta," he called. "Help me clear a path to the tunnel."

The Wizard's glare could have struck Digur dead. He was obviously the last person Inesta wanted to help at the moment, but it was in his best interests, and Digur was certain he could count on the high elf to help save his own life.

Digur began gathering amber mana in his palms and then raised his hands over his head and sprayed the energy over the morga. As the energy spread out in the air, it transformed into fist-sized stones that fell back to ground, pelting the morga about their heads and shoulders. A half-dozen fell to the stone floor, unconscious or dead.

Almost immediately after Digur's hailstones thinned the crowd of morga, he saw a line of lightning arc its way through those left standing. The lighting hit each one in turn, making their bodies spasm and convulse as they were added to the chain.

When lightning erupted from the chest of the fourth morga in the chain, Digur knew he was in trouble. The line of lightning became a dot as it raced straight toward him. When it hit, the lightning burned into his chest and made him convulse involuntarily.

Luckily most of the energy had been consumed as the chain passed through the morga, so Digur suffered only a minor burn. He smiled through gritted teeth at Inesta, who just shrugged.

Digur calmed his rage and focused on the task at hand. Their two spells had cleared out most of the morga, so the dwarf moved toward his companions, dispatching another morga along the way with his force blade.

Lithann had summoned a bobcat and a lizard, and was busy picking off morga with her bow. Inesta's lightning armor had burned several of the monsters, which lay twitching on the ground around him. The rest were keeping their distance.

"Keep them off me for a minute," said Digur as he reached his friends. "I have a plan."

"We'll do our best," said Lithann as she dropped another charging morga with an arrow that sailed past its mandibles, through its mouth, and out the back of its head.

Inesta didn't say a word to Digur, but turned back toward the pit and began casting a spell.

Digur took that as the Wizard's way of agreeing, and set about executing his plan. In quick succession, he conjured two walls of stone, one on either side of them, running from the pit to the wall on either side of the tunnel.

"That will slow them down a bit," he said as he began summoning a thoughtspore in the air above the stone wall channel. As soon as his amorphous familiar formed above him, Digur opened his mind to the creature and mentally transferred an incantation to it that would help keep the path clear.

After giving the flying spore a few simple commands to follow, Digur turned his attention back to the pit for the final piece of the plan.

That's when he saw what spell the Wizard had cast. Inesta had conjured a cloud of greenish-yellow gas on top of the pit. The morga caught in the roiling cloud clutched at their throats and fell to their knees, their mandibles clicking rapidly as white foamy phlegm dribbled out of their mouths.

"You call that helping?" asked Digur, pointing at the cloud of poison gas.

"I call it covering our escape," said Inesta, and he began striding toward the tunnel.

"You're not escaping!" yelled Digur.

It was a reflex. Digur didn't even think about what he was doing. He just flung his hands forward in rage and unleashed the mana he'd gathered for the wall spell. A thick stream of energy shot from Digur's palms and bashed into Inesta with such force that it flung the Wizard back into the poisonous cloud and over the edge of the pit.

*****

"Digur!" yelled Lithann. She looked back and forth between the cloud and the dwarf. "What have you done?"

"He was going to betray us!" said Digur. "Leave him to his precious morga. I have a bridge to build." Lithann could see him gathering more mana in his hands.

This was wrong, and Lithann knew it. Even if the Sortilege mage had planned to betray them, leaving him to die a horrible, painful death at the claws of the morga was morally wrong.

"Think about your brother," she said before Digur could drop a wall on top of the Wizard. "Would you really condemn someone to the same fate he suffered?"

"If it would save his life?" said Digur. "Yes!"

Lithann shook her head. "I don't believe you. You're not like the Grimhammers and Inestas of this world. I think you're like me. I came down here alone to save Jhonart, and you risked everything, left everything and everyone behind just to help me. You care about people more than you're willing to admit. You've put aside old hatreds to work side-by-side with an enemy of your people for a chance to save a single person from suffering the same fate as your brother. I think every life matters to you, including Inesta's…and mine."

With that, Lithann turned and ran into the poison cloud. She kneeled at the edge of the pit and looked down at Inesta through the roiling gas. He lay unmoving at the bottom of the pit, his eyes open. He didn't even convulse from the poison, even though white foam had begun to form around his lips.

"Inesta!" she called. "Can you move?"

"He's stunned," said Digur, who had kneeled down beside her. "It will wear off."

Lithann felt the poison burning her throat and lungs and began coughing up phlegm and foam. "Place your wall bridge beside us and keep the path clear," she said after the coughing fit subsided. "I'll get Inesta out of there."

She channeled a large ball of mana into her hands and used it to summon her mountain gorilla down in the pit next to the Wizard. She then used the rest of her gathered mana to rouse the great ape from its summoning slumber. "Get him to safety," she commanded the ape.

The gorilla grabbed Inesta's limp body and draped it across his hairy shoulder. As the ape began climbing out of the pit, a horizontal wall of stone appeared next to Lithann. It spanned the pit like a bridge, with just a small step up from the stone floor on either side.

"It's not pretty," said Digur, "but it'll hold. I could have done better with more time."

"It's perfect," said Lithann with a smile.

She actually began to think they might all get out of the arena alive until she turned around.

CHAPTER 12: DOWN AND OUT

By the time the gorilla climbed over the edge of the pit, Inesta had regained control over his body. He couldn't see Lithann or the dwarf through the cloud, which continued to burn at his throat.

He dismissed the poison cloud and tried to drop off the shoulder of the great ape, but it held him tight and turned its head to stare into Inesta's eyes and then grunted. Inesta understood the beast all too well. It wanted to complete its last command, which was to get him to safety, and it wouldn't let anything get in its way, even Inesta.

Resigned to his current fate, Inesta scanned the arena for the others. He spotted them when the gorilla turned toward the tunnel and the safety it offered. They had retreated onto the bridge the dwarf and were completely surrounded. A score of the monsters encircled them both, slashing and swiping at them and driving them to the ground.

The gorilla began loping on three limbs toward the tunnel, dragging Inesta's feet on the stone floor as it moved. Above him, the Wizard could see the walls literally crawling with morga as they streamed down toward the arena floor.

The dwarf's thoughtspore used waves of energy to keep the morga off the stone walls that protected their escape route, while Lithann's lizard and bobcat had retreated to the tunnel entrance and attacked any monsters that reached the floor. But those meager defenses would be overwhelmed soon. Their time was rapidly running out.

A voice inside Inesta told him to ride the gorilla to safety. He'd gotten what he'd come for: verification that Jhonart was the only other wood elf down here. He could leave them all here and let the morga contain the situation for him. And yet...

He had not been able to move in that pit, but he could still see and hear. He'd heard everything Lithann had said to Digur. He'd watched as she entered a cloud of poison he'd conjured in an effort to save his life. He'd seen the dwarf walk into the same cloud to help her.

Inesta had questioned his orders every time he had watched someone die at the hands of the morga, every time he'd allowed someone to blunder into morga territory without a word of warning, every time he'd failed to rescue someone from an advancing horde.

Until he had seen Lithann and Digur venturing into danger together, he had not lifted a finger. He had done what he'd been told, and never voiced his dissent with the leaders of the Sortilege. To do so would have been to sentence himself to death.

But if a dwarf and an elf, racial enemies who patrolled their borders day and night just to keep each other at bay, could work together—could become friends—then maybe his people were wrong about how to handle the morga problem. Maybe he should be doing more than just keeping his people's biggest mistake a secret from the other races.

The urgency of Inesta's situation almost hit him on the head as one of the morga on the wall above the tunnel dislodged a chunk of rock that plummeted past his eyes as the gorilla carried him into the tunnel.

The small voice inside Inesta's psyche said: "They're beyond your help now. Save yourself."

*   *   *   *   *   *

Jhonart raced toward the bridge, commanding his animals to attack the horde surrounding Lithann. He saw Wiley bite down on the ankle of one of the monsters and sever its foot. The monster crumpled to the ground and fell off the bridge as the fox spat out the foot and attacked the next monster.

As Jhonart's creatures waded into the fray, he howled out an incantation that would imbue all of his and Lithann's animals with the ferocity of the wilderness. His ferret, wolf, and lizard snarled, howled, and hissed as they attacked. In the distance, Jhonart heard another hiss, along with a bobcat's yowl, and the thundering growl of a gorilla.

When Jhonart reached the giant scrum, he swung his staff at the first monster he saw, cracking its skull open with a mighty blow. Wiley and his beasts had taken down four more, but Lithann was still surrounded. She and another person—probably the elf Wizard he'd seen earlier—had been forced to the ground, but he could barely see either of them beneath the pile of monsters that kicked and clawed at every exposed patch of flesh.

At this rate, he knew he wouldn't get to them in time, and he'd already used his mass sleep spell. Jhonart had no choice but to keep attacking the monsters one at a time and hope Lithann and her companion could survive until he reached them.

As Jhonart swung his staff again, he saw a bolt of lightning tear through the ranks of the monsters on the bridge. Four of them fell into the pit, looking like the charred remains of a campfire.

He glanced across the bridge and saw the elf Wizard standing there holding a twisting, silver wand. Electricity continued to spark at its tip as the Wizard nodded at Jhonart.

"Let's get your girl and her dwarven friend out of here," he said.

Jhonart wanted to protest that Lithann was not his girl and that she would never be friends with a filthy dwarf, but there was no time for that. Instead, he simply nodded and finished off the monster in front of him with a solid crack to its ribcage that crushed the beast's chest.

A moment later, after another bolt of chain lightning from the Wizard's wand, another solid smack with his staff, and some ferocious attacks from the assembled animals, Lithann and the dwarf had been completely uncovered.

Their beaten and bloodied bodies lay on the stone bridge. The dwarf's face was crisscrossed with deep gashes and his robes were little more than blood-soaked shreds of cloth. He smiled weakly at Jhonart, but made no effort to move.

Lithann's arms lay across her face. They had been almost scraped to the bone both above and below her elbow as she'd used them to protect her face. Wiley licked at her wounds, but when Jhonart looked toward the tunnel, he saw no evidence of the other animals she'd summoned.

Lithann lay perfectly still on the stone bridge, either unconscious or dead.

*　　*　　*　　*　　*　　*

Inesta had used his last teleport of the day to escape the clutches of the gorilla and used it not to escape, but to return to the arena and save Lithann and the dwarf.

He had made the decision in the heat of the moment, and even now questioned his actions. Perhaps in the fullness of time he would realize the folly of sticking his neck out to save two outsiders, but for now, he had no choice but to follow through and finish what he had started.

"Transport Lithann and the dwarf out of this place!" he commanded to Jhonart. "I will clear a path through these vermin."

The ferret turned its head at Inesta's last word and hissed at the Wizard. He ignored the creature and turned toward the tunnel. As he suspected, it had been completely overrun by morga, and more streamed down the wall from the viewing area.

He pointed his wand at the group and unleashed another jagged chain of lightning that tore through the front of the group, dropping four of the approaching horde. The grizzly, wolf, and ferret streaked past Inesta and engaged three more, clearing enough space for what the Wizard planned next.

The emerald tegu ran past him next, moving much quicker than any lizard ought to be able to run, especially with the dead weight of an elf on its back. Wiley ran beside the tegu, protecting her master.

However, when Inesta looked back at the Beastmaster, he saw him striding forward without the dwarf, who still lay on the bridge.

"Get the dwarf!" snarled Inesta. "He's with us."

"Get him yourself," said Jhonart. "I'm not touching any filthy dwarf."

"Dammit!" swore Inesta. "We need him." With no time to argue, Inesta turned toward the fleeing lizard. "Wiley!" he yelled in his most commanding voice, "Guard Digur!"

The fox looked back at him and then glanced up at her master's lifeless form on the back of the lizard. She hesitated a moment and then began racing back toward the bridge.

"Good girl!" said Inesta to the fox as she ran past him. "I certainly hope this works," he added to himself.

Inesta sent another chain of lightning racing along ahead of the retreating Beastmaster and his animals and then sheathed his wand to begin summoning a creature. He was a bit rusty at summoning spells because he rarely used creatures while fighting, but he couldn't take his time because every second counted. Sweat beaded on his forehead as he completed the spell and watched the gargoyle form out of the mist of mana next to him.

The grotesque gray statue stretched huge bat-like wings and flexed bulging stone muscles as it rose into the air beside the Wizard. "Convey the dwarf and fox to safety," commanded Inesta.

As the gargoyle flew off toward the bridge, Inesta checked on Digur one last time before running for the tunnel. The dwarf had rolled over and was trying to push himself up onto his hands and knees as Wiley stood over him.

Luckily none of the morga seemed to be taking any interest in the dwarf. Of course, that meant they were all scrambling toward the tunnel to block the exit. Inesta had one last trick up his sleeve, though.

He caught up to the Beastmaster, who was trying to fight his way through the horde of morga. The dwarf's thoughtspore continued to buffet the tops of the walls with force waves, keeping the morga coming at them from the sides at bay, while Jhonart and his creatures had held the line, but there was simply no way through.

"Pull back," said Inesta. "I will handle this." As Jhonart took a step back, Inesta activated his voltaric shield, an innate ability he had learned as a child, checked to make sure the circle of lightning enchantment he had cast earlier was still functioning, and moved into the middle of the horde.

The first attack glanced off his voltaric shield and the morga ate a bolt of lightning for its trouble, dropping to the ground in a quivering heap as electricity played across its body. Several more monsters attacked Inesta as well, ripping the Wizard's robes in several places and slicing into his skin, but each morga received a massive jolt of lightning in return.

Inesta made it to the middle of the horde, right in front of the tunnel entrance. He was completely surrounded on all sides. More morga scrambled down the wall above him and many had spilled out into the tunnel.

He ignored their attacks as he gathered a sizable amount of mana into his hands. He felt his life draining away with every slash of claws around him, but gritted his teeth and flung his arms to the sides as he completed the spell.

Electricity sprayed from Inesta's fingertips and began weaving and interconnecting until it formed a sphere that encircled his entire body. Then, in a brilliant flash, the ball of electricity exploded, flying away from the Wizard in all directions and electrifying the very air around him.

Every morga within range went rigid as electricity coursed through their bodies. Some burst into flames from the heat, while others shook uncontrollably as electricity searched for a path through their bodies toward a ground state. Most simply froze in place and then dropped to the floor, dead or shaking as residual electricity snaked across their lifeless bodies.

"Now!" said Inesta. "Run!"

Inesta stepped into the tunnel and watched as Jhonart and his creatures, the lizard carrying Lithann, and the gargoyle carrying the dwarf all exited the arena. He then turned and followed.

They were out of the arena, but far from safe.

*   *   *   *   *   *

Jhonart stopped ten meters down the tunnel with the ferret by his side. With Lithann unconscious he needed Sosruko again to see in the dark. He waited for the elf Wizard to catch up.

"I hope you know your way out of here," said Jhonart. Even looking at the world as shadows upon shadows, he could tell that the elf was hurt badly. His torso and legs glistened as a dark liquid had soaked his robes and boots. Truth be told, he was surprised the Wizard was still standing.

"Follow the gargoyle," said the elf. "I am directing it toward our rendezvous point. Can you secure this egress?"

"Put a wall over the arena entrance?" asked Jhonart. "Sure. I can slow down those little monsters a bit."

"Make it so!" said the Wizard. "Our dwarf is incapacitated at the moment."

As Jhonart conjured a wall of thorns that would at least slow down their pursuit, he wondered where Lithann had picked up this strange elf. He certainly wasn't from the Straywood, and probably not from Wychwood or Bitterwood either. That meant he was either Atalancia or Sortilege, which amounted to the same thing in Jhonart's book—snooty elves who revered magic above nature.

Jhonart humphed as he turned to follow the Wizard before the elf disappeared into the blackness. "A snooty high elf and a dirty dwarf," said Jhonart to himself. "That girl will socialize with anyone. She's like a butterfly flitting between flowers and weeds. She doesn't care where she lands."

The elf Wizard followed a long, winding course through a maze of tunnels. It didn't take long for Jhonart to become completely turned around and lost. Even if he'd wanted to return to the arena, he had no idea how to get there.

Twice along their journey, the high elf stopped and dropped a fog bank behind them to cover an intersection. Eventually, they arrived at a huge cavern. Jhonart couldn't see the ceiling through the ferret's eyes, let alone the other side of the cavern, but looking back, he could see two other tunnel entrances flanking the one they ran out of.

"This doesn't look safe," he said.

"It is most definitely not," said the elf. "Arrange your creatures in a semi-circle around us, and be ready to block those tunnels if I'm interrupted."

"What are you going to do?" asked Jhonart.

"Transport us to a safe location," replied the Wizard.

Jhonart hated taking orders, especially from a near-dead high elf. In a straight-up fight, Jhonart knew he could take this fancy-robed high elf. Seeing no other option to get to safety, though, he complied.

Sosruko alternately watched the tunnels and the Wizard so Jhonart could see what was happening. The gargoyle landed next to the Wizard and laid down the dwarf and the fox.

"Give me my wand and hold onto the fox," said the Wizard.

Jhonart was about to protest that he didn't have a wand when he saw the dwarf raise his hand weakly toward the elf and hand him a long rod. He then hugged Wiley, which made Jhonart want to attack him. No one touches a Beastmaster's pet!

A moment later, the wand flashed in the Wizard's hand and both Wiley and the dwarf disappeared with a loud popping sound. The gargoyle flew over and took up a guarding position above Jhonart.

"What in Infernia did you do to them?" he asked.

"Teleported them to safety," said the elf. "Be quiet while I work. Our lives depend on the rapidity of my actions."

Jhonart humphed again and turned around. He thought he had heard scratching noises coming from the tunnel entrance they had run out of. He sent Sosruko toward the entrance to see. Sure enough, the ferret saw creatures moving in the darkness.

He quickly conjured another wall of thorns. It wouldn't block the tunnel, but it would slow them down and make life very painful for those monsters.

Behind him, Jhonart heard another popping sound as the first few creatures came through the thorny wall of vines. The gargoyle dove and punched one of the monsters with its stony, clawed hand, driving the creature's head into the ground with a loud crack.

"You're next," said the elf behind him.

Before he could even protest, Jhonart felt his body begin to fold in on itself. It was an incredibly unpleasant feeling, like falling and being punched in the gut at the same time.

A moment later, Jhonart found himself completely in the dark. He concentrated on his ferret and could still see what was going on in the cavern, but he knew he was somewhere else because the sounds of battle he had heard a second earlier now sounded muffled, as if they were coming through a wall.

He saw the Wizard being surrounded by the monsters. The wolf and grizzly had disappeared, but the lizard and gargoyle fought on. A dozen of the beasts that had kidnapped Jhonart surrounded the high elf and slashed at him with their claws, sending the Wizard to his knees.

The gargoyle swooped down, grabbed the Wizard by the arm, and flew up into the air, getting hit several times before it rose above the horde. Just as the gargoyle flew the Wizard out of Sosruko's sight range, the Wizard's wand flashed and Jhonart heard twin popping sounds: one through the wall and one in the darkness behind Jhonart.

At that point, the monsters turned on Sosruko and Jhonart's view of the huge chamber went dark.

CHAPTER 13: STRAINED ALLEGIANCES

Lithann awoke on a cold, stone floor and stared up at the face of Jhonart who stood above her looking at something she couldn't see. Worry lines crisscrossed his furrowed forehead and his lips were set in a determined, grim frown.

"Hi," she said, weakly. "You're safe."

Jhonart looked down at her and grinned, the twinkle in his eyes returning as he unfurrowed his brow. "Welcome back," he said. "We weren't sure you would pull through."

A wet nose nuzzled her neck and Lithann felt hot breath on her face. She reached up to ruffle Wiley's ears and saw bandages covering her arms.

"How bad was it?" she asked as pain cascaded down both arms from her shoulders to her wrists. She lay her arms carefully back on the cool floor.

"Bad," said Jhonart. "I have a few healing spells remaining if you feel up to it. Growing new skin, even with magic, will be a painful process."

"Is everyone else okay?" Lithann tried to sit up, but without using her arms, it was nearly impossible.

"I have tended to my own injuries," said Inesta as he strode into Lithann's view. His robes were in tatters and caked with dried blood. "However, I exhausted my meager supply of healing magic in the process."

"And Digur?" asked Lithann, hoping for the best but fearing the worst, as no one had yet volunteered any information about her dwarven friend.

"The dwarf remains unconscious," said Inesta. He looked as if he wanted to say more on the matter, but changed the subject instead. "Now that you are conscious, we can move you to the bed. It seemed prudent to tend to your wounds as quickly as possible upon our return to the safety of my chamber."

Lithann had begun to suspect they had returned to the Wizard's isolated cavern. She had heard the waterfall running into the pool of water behind her and could smell the musty odor of books and papers, which she knew filled the chamber.

She returned to the subject of healing Digur. "Jhonart," she said. "Please use the rest of your healing magic on Digur."

Jhonart's smile faded and his bright, sparkling eyes narrowed and darkened into charcoal pits. "No," he said. "I will not heal a filthy dwarf."

"He's my friend," protested Lithann. She gritted her teeth and pushed her arms against the stone floor to sit up, nearly fainting from the excruciating pain shooting through her limbs. "He helped save your life."

"Are you certain of that?" protested Jhonart. "I saw him force push Inesta here into the arena. That doesn't sound very friendly to me."

Inesta shook his head. "The dwarf and I had a minor disagreement over tactics," he said. "I assure you I harbor no ill will against him for his actions."

Jhonart crossed his arms. "Look. No offense to you, Inesta. You might be a fine person for a high elf, but I don't know you and I don't know this dwarf either. We wood elves take care of our own."

He looked down at Lithann, widened his eyes, and nodded his head once, as if demanding she agree with him.

"I take care of my friends," said Lithann. She paused while completing the long, painful process of pushing herself to her feet. "And at this moment, I'm beginning to wonder if I can actually count any wood elves among that group."

Lithann scanned the room looking for Digur. She found him lying near the pool. It seemed that someone—probably Inesta—had at least washed and dressed his wounds. The dwarf's face was almost completely covered in bandages while a wide swath of bloodstained, white cloth had been wrapped around his torso.

"I will tend to my friend," she said to Jhonart. "You go ahead and save your healing spells for someone you actually care about: yourself."

Jhonart shrugged and threw his arms up in the air before turning and stalking over to a corner of the chamber, where he sat down against the wall.

Lithann walked slowly and deliberately over toward Digur's still form. Every step was torture as the newly-healed muscles, tendons, and flesh flexed and shifted against one another under her bandages.

She kneeled down beside Digur, channeled mana into her hands, and began the first of many healing incantations.

*   *   *   *   *   *

"I saw what you did back in the arena," said Digur some time later.

The dwarf sat at Inesta's table while the elf stood nearby. Lanterns lit most of the chamber, although Digur didn't need them to see. Lithann had fallen asleep on the bed with Wiley lying next to the elf, one eye open to watch the proceedings at the table.

Jhonart had also fallen asleep in a dark corner of the chamber, beside the Wizard's trunks. Lithann's Beastmaster friend had not said a word to either Digur or Inesta since the dwarf had regained consciousness.

He was an enigma to Digur, still more of a goal to be accomplished than an actual person. Perhaps that was for the best. The last thing Digur wanted to do was to come between his new friend and her old friend.

"I carried through on my promise to help Lithann save her friend," said Inesta. "Nothing more."

He stared at the desk while speaking, as if examining some important piece of paper, although Digur suspected the Wizard simply couldn't look him in the eye.

"You keep telling yourself that and maybe you'll even believe it someday," said Digur, trying not to smile too broadly. "But you and me both know the truth."

"What truth is that, my dwarf friend?" asked Inesta as he studiously picked up a piece of paper and ran his finger across the text, as if checking a piece of information.

"That you had a change of heart," said Digur. "You could have saved your own skin and left us there to die. Instead, you came back and almost single-handedly saved all of our skins."

"I am certain you or Lithann would have done the same for me," said Inesta, as he dropped the piece of paper and looked directly into Digur's eyes, perhaps to study the dwarf's reaction.

Digur laughed and immediately regretted it as his chest tightened and sent a stabbing pain right through his ribcage.

"I'm sure Lithann would have done the same back there," said Digur after the pain subsided. "As for me, I might not have then, but I would now.

You're okay, for a fancy-dressing high elf."

Inesta bowed. "I am not so sure my superiors would agree with you, but I will deal with that when the time comes. He then snapped his fingers. "Aha!" he said. "Speaking of vestments, I have some items you may be able to use."

The Wizard walked over to his chests and began rooting around in the bottom of one of them. "As you may have noticed, the morga have little use for clothing or armor, or even magical items and gear."

Inesta pulled various objects out of the chest and dropped them on the floor. Digur saw leather boots and gauntlets, a shining scimitar, an enormous hammer, a box filled with amulets and rings, and what looked like a dragonscale hauberk. Almost all the gear was undoubtedly of dwarven manufacture, and Digur was certain he recognized a couple of pieces.

"Here it is!" he said eventually as he pulled a set of dwarf-sized Forcemaster robes out of the chest. Inesta brought the folded robes over to the table and placed them in front of Digur.

"You cannot venture home looking like that," added the Wizard as Digur stared at the clothes.

"How…how did you get this?" he asked. A thousand emotions raced around his head and through his heart all vying to be the first to cross the threshold between his body and the room.

"I…" started Inesta, and then trailed off. It was the first time Digur had seen the Wizard at a loss for words. "I found them," he said finally. "Part of my duties are—were—to clean up after the morga."

"To make sure no evidence was ever found, right?" said Digur, keeping his emotions in check for the moment. He didn't even look at the Wizard for fear that seeing the high elf's guilty face would unleash the torrent of rage welling up deep inside him.

"You knew the dwarf who wore these," said Inesta. It was a statement rather than a question.

"These are my brother's robes," said Digur, quietly. Then the dam broke inside. "My brother!" he yelled. "Did you watch him die? Did you sit back in your hidey hole and watch my brother die, you miserable sack of dirt?"

Wiley yelped behind Digur, and the dwarf heard both Lithann and Jhonart start awake as he continued to yell. "You bring these demons down upon us and you watch them kill innocent people, and then you clean up their messes so no one finds out what you've done!"

Digur pushed the chair over as he stood and then climbed up onto the table, trampling and scattering papers as he walked across to stand face to face with Inesta.

"You and your Sortilege masters are the real demons!" he screamed, his face centimeters away from Inesta's. "My brother was a good person. He didn't deserve the fate that you and yours brought down upon him. He sacrificed his life to save me. He died to save me!"

"And Inesta nearly died while saving us," said Lithann softly, as she came up beside Digur. She took his trembling hands in hers, turned him away from the Wizard, and looked him deep in the eyes.

"We owe Inesta our lives," she said. "You know that. And whatever he was when we first met him, he's a different elf now. I can see the change inside of him."

"He watched my brother die," said Digur softly, weakly, like a small child crying to his mother about a dead pet.

"Maybe he did and maybe he didn't," said Lithann. "You haven't even given him a breath to explain."

She turned him back toward Inesta. "Give him a chance," she continued. "That's what friends do."

Jhonart chuckled over in the corner. "So, we're all friends now?" he said. "That's a laugh!"

"You keep out of this!" snapped Lithann. "This does not concern you. It is between me and my two friends."

Digur took another deep breath to calm down, and found the pain in his chest did a reasonable job of diverting his attention from his rage. He looked at Inesta for the first time since his blood had risen to the point where he could no longer see straight. He had to admit the Wizard looked visibly shaken. His eyes were moist around the edges and he stared at the floor as Digur regarded him.

"I will give him a chance to speak," said Digur calmly. "But if I don't like what he has to say, I am leaving and telling every dwarf I trust about what is really going on down here."

"What exactly is going on down here?" asked a high, lilting voice from the other side of the room.

Digur's head snapped to the side, all his ebbing rage turning into adrenalin. Two high-elven Wizards stood in front of the waterfall dressed in the same gold-lined purple robes Inesta wore.

"Please, Inesta," said the Sortilege Wizard. "Tell us what exactly you are doing with these interlopers?"

*   *   *   *   *   *

Inesta felt all the eyes in the chamber staring at him, waiting to see how he reacted to the arrival of the two Sortilege mages.

The female who had challenged him was his immediate superior, Vanova. Inesta had never once seen her smile. She had a long, gaunt face, with high deep-set cheeks, and a straight, thin nose that looked a bit like an arrowhead. She always wore her gray hair pulled back into a bun on the back of her head, which made her stern features look even more severe.

Vanova had sent Inesta to this posting shortly after he and she had engaged in a very public, heated argument over the best course of action to take in dealing with the morga. As his superior, Vanova had no problems pulling the necessary strings to send her chief rival off to a distant post where he could no longer make waves.

Inesta had vowed to find the answer to containing the morga problem, which was why he had kept such meticulous notes. But he knew he could never return to Sortilege until he had found a viable solution. Vanova would see to that as long as she lived.

If it had only been Vanova here in his chamber, Inesta wouldn't have even hesitated. He'd wished for this opportunity for a long time, trapped down in the dark away from the stars, away from his people.

However, Vanova was smart enough not to come alone, and smart enough to bring Limesi with her. The second Wizard also had the sharp cheeks and nasal features common among Inesta's people, but he almost always wore a smile. Even now Limesi had a bit of a smirk on his face.

Inesta could only guess at what private joke Limesi was laughing at inside; probably he was thinking that this was another fine mess that Inesta had gotten them into. The two of them had been inseparable during their apprenticeships and had braved a lot of trouble together over the years.

Limesi was the closest thing Inesta had ever had to a brother.

CHAPTER 14: AT WHAT COST

Inesta glanced around the room to gauge the reactions of Lithann and her friends to the sudden appearance of his Sortilege companions. Lithann had backed up a step and laid a hand on Wiley's head, while Jhonart leaned against the wall in the corner, seemingly unconcerned.

Digur, though, had balled his hands into fists, which twitched tightly against his body. Inesta's keen eyes noticed that the dwarf's right hand inched ever so slowly toward the hilt of his force blade. If he was going to defuse this situation, he had to act fast.

The elf plastered his most welcoming smile across his face and turned back toward his visitors. "Welcome, Limesi," he said brightly. "It is good to see you after so long an absence."

Then, almost as an afterthought, and with his smile fading just slightly, Inesta added: "Hello, Vanova. What has brought you here to my humble hole in the ground?"

"You know all too well why I am here," said Vanova. Her tone was so cold that ice could have formed on her words. "You were told to contain this situation, and as usual you have failed to follow my orders."

"But I have followed your orders," said Inesta, "to the letter." As he spoke to Vanova, the Wizard stared at Limesi, trying to connect emotionally with his old friend.

"As you can see, they are contained," he said. "They cannot leave this chamber. Our secrets are safe."

Even as he said it, Inesta knew he had made a mistake.

"How much do they know?" demanded Vanova. "How much have you told them?"

She looked at the note-filled table behind Inesta with the eradication charts and morga anatomy diagram plainly visible on top. "Do you know what the punishment is for divulging Sortilege secrets to outsiders?" she asked. "There are worse places I can banish you to. How long would you last alone in the Darkfenne?"

"Vanova," interrupted Limesi. He placed a hand on her arm. "Let him explain before you pass judgment and pronounce his sentence."

"Thank you, brother," said Inesta. He looked Limesi deep in the eyes, hoping to see some indication that his friend would stand with him should it come to it. However, Limesi had learned long ago how to mask his emotions, which is how he had risen so fast among their peers while Inesta's career had languished.

"I have not divulged any secrets that cannot be contained," continued Inesta. "While at first I planned to follow your suggestion and allow the morga to have them and then clean up the mess afterward, I believe they can be of use to us."

"These lower races a help to us?" she asked. "How? As slaves?"

"I would not state it that way," said Inesta, "but in a word, yes."

Lithann and the others gasped at this. Inesta turned toward them and yelled, "Silence! Your betters are talking!" while at the same time, he winked. He hoped they all saw it...and believed it.

"These two," he said, pointing at the two Beastmasters, "are good in a fight, and they cannot leave here without the help of the dwarf. They are contained, and if they wish to live, they will comply."

"The nine hells they will!" growled Digur.

Inesta pulled out his elemental wand, which still had chain lightning imbued within its twisting silver shaft, and pointed it at Digur. "This one we can send back to the dwarves. They already know about the morga and have walled themselves off from the threat."

Inesta stared hard at Digur, trying to reach out to him and show the dwarf that he understood his life all too well. "I have monitored the dwarven situation closely and I assure you that the Anvil Throne elders will not listen to the ramblings of this poor, crazy dwarf. He is an outcast already. Sending him back would be a worse fate than death. Believe me, I know."

Inesta and Digur stared at each other for a moment longer, and the Wizard thought he saw a tear begin to form in the dwarf's eye and slip down into the bandages covering his face.

The Wizard quickly turned back toward Vanova and Limesi to keep their attention on him. "So, as you see, I have the situation completely under control. I do not require any assistance in this matter."

Inesta hoped it had been enough. He knew his impromptu explanation sounded flimsy and was certain that if Vanova were here alone, she would take a hard line.

He looked to Limesi, and noticed that Vanova was also now staring at Inesta's old friend. It all came down to him.

"It is very unorthodox," said Limesi, noncommittally.

Inesta's heart fell into his stomach. He had hoped for a more supportive statement from his former bunkmate.

"You know how I feel about loose ends," said Vanova. "Tell me your thoughts, Limesi. How should we proceed?"

"In the end," began Limesi, "we must always put the safety of Sortilege first in all endeavors. I believe the proposal put forth by Inesta is untenable. The only rational course of action is to eliminate all threats as they arise."

Inesta noticed that his friend had stopped short of actually giving the elimination order. Perhaps he thought that would absolve him from the blame and rage that Inesta would direct at those responsible for making him kill his new friends, but it didn't matter. His brother had not stood with him when it counted. He had sealed his fate.

"Eliminate them," said Vanova. She raised a wand of her own and pointed it at Inesta. "Now!"

"As you wish," said Inesta.

He turned and raised his own wand toward Digur again, while at the same time he began counting down from five with his other hand, which he held against the front of his robe, hidden from Vanova and Limesi.

At zero, Inesta whirled around, pointed his wand at his biggest political enemy and his oldest friend in the world, and unleashed the chain lightning spell imbued within.

*   *   *   *   *   *

Chaos erupted in the small chamber as Inesta's lightning bolt tore through the two Sortilege Wizards. Digur knew they all had to work together and finish this battle quickly. None of their group had healed completely after the morga battle in the arena.

When Inesta began counting down, Digur had begun channeling mana into his right hand behind his back. When the Wizard turned, the dwarf stepped to the side and whipped his clenched fist forward to fling a rock made of magical energy.

As Inesta's lightning bounced from Vanova to Limesi, singing their robes and causing the bun on the female elf's tightly-bound hair to explode with static electricity, the rock Digur had thrown grew in size to become a flying boulder that arced into the air, bounced off the stone ceiling, and crash down on top of Vanova.

The boulder staggered the elf Wizard and left a long gash across her forehead. She stumbled backward and slipped into the pool beneath the waterfall.

Almost immediately after Vanova stepped into the pool, it seemed to erupt in a geyser. At first Digur wondered how the small splash from her misstep had grown so large, but then he recognized it as the spell Lithann had used to quench the flames in the temple. That seemed so long ago now.

The geyser drenched the Sortilege Wizard and left her gasping for air. While Vanova coughed up red-tinged water, and wiped a mixture of blood and frizzed-out hair from her eyes, Wiley leapt on the female elf and sunk her teeth into Vanova's cheek. The elf screamed as the fox dropped to the ground with a large flap of skin hanging off her canines.

"So, that's how this is going to be, is it?" asked Vanova as she stepped back out of the pool.

She was drenched from head to toe and bled from a gash in her fore-head and a gaping wound in her check. Her robes had a massive, char-lined hole and the blistered skin underneath oozed a viscous, white liquid. However, a fire burned in her eyes. "Excellent," she continued. "I've been waiting for this day for a long time!"

Vanova kindled balls of mana in both hands, which burst into flames. She then thrust her arms out to each side as she spun around, sending rings of flames spiraling out from her body. In seconds, the entire room ig-nited, burning everyone except the female Wizard and setting fire to Inesta's notes and bed.

Even Limesi screamed as the ring of fire enveloped him and set his robes alight.

Digur cringed as fire washed over him, burning his clothes and skin and hair. After the flame wave washed hover him, Digur was alarmed to see the cloth bandages surrounding his chest and face had begun to smolder. He worked feverishly to unwrap the bandages before the cloth began to burn his already wounded flesh.

As Digur removed his bandages and patted out small fires on his tattered robes, he heard Lithann begin a conjuration beside him. He turned just in time to see a large tree grow out of the stone floor in the open space where the two of them had slept during their first night in this chamber.

As the magical branches spread out across the ceiling of the chamber and sprouted leaves, Digur began to feel his health improve. His chest ached a little less, his burned flesh began to cool, and his weariness started to subside.

Just then, the male elf, Limesi, who had not yet attacked the group and had only taken damage from Inesta's chain lightning and Vanova's ring of fire, spread his arms out wide, the singed sleeves of his robe still smoldering as bright, white mana began to form in his palms.

"Enough!" he yelled as the mana exploded in a blinding flash of brilliant white light.

Digur clutched at his eyes as pain seared through them into his brain. He fell to his knees, dazed by the power of the attack. When he opened his eyes, Digur found he couldn't see anything; white spots dotted his vision, crowding out all other images.

* * * * * *

"Why do you fight us, brother?" asked Limesi.

Lithann had fallen to her hands and knees after the flash of light, but found she could move and see a little. After checking on Digur, who had put out the flames licking at his clothes but seemed out of it otherwise, she crawled behind the table. She looked up and saw the parchment littered top was ablaze, sending clouds of smoke up to the ceiling where it pooled and grew in volume. They would all suffocate soon if the fire continued to burn.

"We cannot murder innocent people in our efforts to hide our shame, brother," she heard Inesta reply. "If we follow that road, we become no better than the very monsters we created. Can you not see that?"

Lithann peeked around the edge of the table and noticed that along with Digur, Vanova also seemed to have been stunned by the flash of light. She scanned for Wiley and saw her fox lying motionless on the stone floor behind the Sortilege mages. She hoped the fox had just been stunned and that the tree of life could rejuvenate her pet before any more mass attacks were unleashed in the chamber.

"What would you have us do?" asked Limesi. "Return to Sortilege and allow you to reveal all our secrets to the world? The other nations would hunt us down and eradicate us."

Lithann could see this argument would not go their way, and knew they had to plan their next steps. She glanced back at Jhonart, who had hidden in the corner behind Inesta's chests, and got his attention. She pointed at him, spun her finger in the air, and then pointed at herself, which was the Beastmaster signal for "follow my lead."

"I honestly don't care what Vanova does," said Inesta. "She can continue to live as a hateful, power-hungry witch back in the conclave or she can die a horrible, painful death here."

Lithann gathered a large amount of mana in her hands and began summoning Cervere, the Forest Shadow, the black panther she had used in the Anvil Throne arena. After the shadowy cat formed beside her, Lithann imbued the legendary panther with an enchantment that gave it the strength of a bear.

"However, I do not wish to see you hurt, Limesi," continued Inesta. "I had hoped you would see the folly of Vanova's ways and work with me."

Lithann looked back at Jhonart, who had summoned his own legendary creature, the great, black, alpha wolf named Redclaw. Its eyes glowed even in the lantern-lit room, but its thick, black fur seemed to drink in all light.

"That's not going to happen, brother," replied Limesi behind her.

Lithann curled her fingertips and brought them together to form a cage, and then pointed at Jhonart and motioned to the left with her thumb and pointed to herself and motioned to the right. She hoped he understood her pantomime, because she had to turn and watch for the right moment to spring into action.

"So be it," said Inesta.

Lithann heard the crack of lightning as the chamber flashed beyond the table. She ordered Cervere to attack Vanova before rolling out from behind the table and conjuring vines to entangle the female Wizard.

At the same time, Jhonart's wolf loped around the other side of the table, and Lithann saw vines appear beneath Limesi's feet and begin wrapping around his legs, torso, and arms.

After casting her spell, Lithann stood up, pulled out her bow and nocked an arrow. The fire on the table had almost completely consumed all the parchment, but the cloud of smoke above them all had billowed down almost to head height.

*　　*　　*　　*　　*　　*

When Digur's vision finally cleared, he surveyed the room and sized up the situation. They had the upper hand in terms of numbers and power, but all of them, including himself and Wiley, were one or two attacks away from unconsciousness. If even one of them went down now, the tide could turn.

Lithann's tree seemed to be rejuvenating everyone slowly, but none of them had any real healing magic left. Digur surmised they really just needed to survive the next few attacks to win, and he knew how to ensure that outcome.

He started by placing a forcefield around his body to make sure he survived long enough to protect everyone. Next, he cast an enchantment on Inesta that would trigger the next time he was attacked.

By the time Digur had completed his first two protection spells, the Beastmasters' legendary creatures had reached the two entangled mages and attacked. The panther stood up on its back legs and swiped at Vanova's shoulders while burying its teeth in her neck. The wolf leapt through the air, its mouth gaping wide, and while it missed the Wizard's jugular, it chomped down hard on Limesi's chest, tearing out skin, flesh, and even a hunk of rib over the elf's heart.

Limesi screamed and fired a lightning bolt point-blank at the wolf as it landed. The beast yelped as its fur singed and electricity coursed through and over its body. But the canine didn't drop. Instead it turned and growled at the Wizard.

For her part, Vanova's blood lust for Inesta remained apparent in her eyes and her actions. Ignoring the panther that had nearly ripped out her throat, she instead ignited another ball of mana in her hand. This time, instead of flinging waves of fire throughout the room, she hurled the flaming ball of mana directly at Inesta.

Just before the fireball impacted the Wizard, though, Digur's enchantment flared to life. Instead of hitting Inesta, the ball of flame bounced off a shimmering shield that appeared around Inesta. The fireball changed direction and flew back toward Vanova in an unerring arc, exploding in a fiery conflagration around the Sortilege female.

When the flames died away, Vanova was quite obviously dead. The fireball had burned away all of her hair, most of her robes, and large sections of her skin, leaving only charred and pink muscle, a bloody skull, and horrible, wide-open eyes that stared out of blackened eye sockets.

"You'll all die for this," said Limesi.

"I don't think so, lad!" said Digur, as he noticed Wiley stirring behind the Sortilege mage. The fox looked like death warmed over, but the dwarf knew the little vixen would fight to the last for her master.

Luckily, Digur could make sure she didn't have to. He cast another one of his numerous protective enchantments around the fox and then cast the same spell on Lithann, just in case.

*   *   *   *   *   *

When the fireball rebounded on Vanova and finished her off, Inesta felt a mixture of emotions: relief and elation at having finally bested his nearly lifelong adversary, but also shock and loss at the death of a fellow high elf. Sortilege was a conclave of exiles. The loss of even one member diminished them all.

The shock of her death and its unexpected impact on Inesta turned the next moments into a blur in his head.

With Vanova down, all of the Beastmaster's creatures turned to attack Limesi.

The panther and wolf dug their claws and teeth deep into Limesi's flesh, ripping, slashing, and tearing chunks of flesh off his torso and legs. Wiley leapt up from behind the Wizard and latched onto the back of his neck.

With strength that Inesta had never seen the fox wield before, she tore out a huge chunk of Limesi's neck, severing his jugular in the process.

"No!" yelled Inesta, as his oldest friend in the world began bleeding out. "Stop!" he screamed.

But it was too late. From behind him, Inesta heard the twang of a bowstring and the high-pitched whistle of an arrow flying through the air. Lithann's aim, as always, was straight and true. Her arrow struck the gaping chest wound inflicted on Limesi by the wolf and pierced his unprotected heart.

He fell limp in the vines encasing his body as blood poured out of his neck and chest and began pooling on the floor.

Inesta ran to his friend and held him, wrapping his arms around his brother as the light in his eyes flickered and died. As Lithann and Digur came up behind him and rested their hands on his shoulders, the exiled

Sortilege Wizard cried softly over the loss of his countryman, his friend, his brother.

Above them, the cloud of smoke threatened to consume the rest of the breathable air in the chamber.

"Maybe we should leave," said Jhonart behind the trio.

EPILOGUE: BRIGHT MORNING

Lithann shielded her eyes from the bright sunshine overhead. After spending more than two days underground, the light was almost blinding.

After the battle, the four of them had doused the fire, teleported out of Inesta's chamber, and climbed two vertical shafts to the relative safety of the rocky foothills where Jhonart had first encountered the morga. Digur then used his Forcemaster abilities to shove a bunch of the large boulders strewn around the area down into the giant hole to seal it up.

Lithann wanted nothing more than to retreat to the safety of the trees where the foliage would filter the sunlight and provide some shade from its unrelenting brilliance. However, she knew there must be wood elf patrols nearby, and they would not react kindly if faced with a dwarf and Sortilege high elf.

"Well, I guess this is where we part ways," said Jhonart. He extended his hand to Inesta. "Thank you for everything. I'm sorry about your friend."

The tall, gaunt Wizard smiled wanly before reaching out and grasping the Beastmaster's hand. "He chose his side and I chose mine," he said. "It could not have ended otherwise."

Jhonart nodded. After a moment, he took a deep breath and extended his hand to Digur as well. "My thanks to you, too, dwarf, for taking care of Lithann and helping to save my life."

"She's the one who saved me," said Digur. "I was lost before Lithann came into my life...and burned down my temple." He smiled and winked at Lithann.

Lithann smiled back at Digur, and a warmth beyond what she felt from the sun's rays spread through her body.

"Well, I guess this is goodbye," said Jhonart. "Lithann and I should return to town and tell our people about what happened here—warn them about these morga of yours."

"No," said Lithann and Inesta at the same time.

"What?" asked Jhonart. "Why?" He looked back and forth between Lithann and Inesta.

The two of them stared at each other for a moment before Lithann shrugged. "You first," she said.

Inesta turned back toward Jhonart. "You can't tell anyone the truth about the morga or the part that I played in your rescue. If news of this intelligence breach reaches the Sortilege conclave, you would put yourself and everyone you love at risk."

"We have to take precautions," said Jhonart. "What if there are more attacks, more abductions?"

"Spread the word about the danger," said Inesta. "Just don't name the morga and don't mention the Sortilege. Keep your warnings vague. Say something like: 'A danger lurks beneath us and we must all be vigilant.'"

Jhonart nodded. "Fine," he said with a chuckle. He smiled and pointed at Lithann. "Your dirty little secrets are safe with us."

"I am concerned with your safety," said Inesta, "all of you. There are many like Vanova in the conclave who will stop at nothing to maintain this secret."

"We will bear that in mind, won't we Lithann," said Jhonart. He turned and smiled at her. "So, now are you ready to go home? I'm sure these two are tired of you by now."

"I'm not going back to the Straywood," replied Lithann. She pushed on before Jhonart could cut her off and tell her what a silly girl she was. "I don't fit in there. I realize that now. It's time for me to move on and find a place where I do belong."

"You're a wood elf and a Beastmaster," said Jhonart. "Where else would you belong other than in the forest? Come home, you silly girl. You'll feel different after a good night's sleep in your own bed."

"I do feel different," said Lithann. "For the first time in my life I feel confident and alive. It's like I've woken up to a bright morning filled with options and opportunities. I can't go back to yesterday. It's time for me to move forward."

"But—" began Jhonart, reaching forward to put his hand on Lithann's shoulder.

"Goodbye, Jhonart," she said as she brushed his hand aside.

It was hard for her to believe that only a few days ago she would have melted into that tender touch, had even sought it out as a way to somehow complete her life. Now, she knew she didn't need to lose herself in someone else to be whole. She needed friends she could count on to stand beside her, not stand in her way.

"It's time for you to go." Lithann pointed toward the forest just visible beyond the boulder. "Warn our people about the coming danger. Guard Straywood from the real enemy."

Jhonart looked like he might yet make another argument, but after looking Lithann in the eye for a moment, his gaze fell away and he turned and walked toward the edge of the Great Forest. Perhaps he saw the resilience in her eyes—something he certainly had never seen before. Perhaps he assumed she would come back to him someday. It didn't matter to Lithann. She was free.

*　*　　*　　*　　*　　*

"Where will you go?" asked Inesta after Jhonart melded into the trees.

"I can answer that," said Digur. "Lithann and I have decided to travel to Victoria and try our hands at the grand arena."

"We make a good team," said Lithann.

"But what of your people?" asked Inesta, looking at Digur. "They are in the most danger from the morga."

Thoughts of his brother darkened Digur's mind a bit and he wiped his eyes with the back of his hands before continuing. "Aye," he said. "You're right about that. But I've dug that hole before and got tossed into it for my troubles. They know the dangers and there's nothing I can do to change their minds about what to do with that knowledge. If they ever decide to fight the morga, I'll return and fight by their sides. I owe my brother that, but I owe the rest of them nothing."

A silence descended over the three of them for a few minutes as Digur reflected on his decision to leave his home and life behind him. He glanced down at his new robes—his brother's robes—and smiled. As long as he lived and remembered his brother, then Dargur would still live, if only in Digur's heart.

"So, what about you?" asked Digur, looking up at Inesta after a time and breaking the silence. He had to shade his eyes against the sun, which had turned the tall elf into an almost pitch-black silhouette. "Why don't you come with us? You're pretty handy in a fight yourself."

"I find I would like that," replied Inesta. "I believe I would like that very much. However, my task here is incomplete."

"You're going back down there?" asked Digur "Why?"

"I have given the matter much thought," said Inesta. "For one thing, I must clean up the mess we left behind. Others will follow Vanova and Limesi. If they find their dead bodies in my chamber, they will hunt me down. That will not only put my life in danger, but yours as well, and that I will not allow to happen."

"We can run," said Lithann. "We can change our names and make a new life for ourselves in Victoria."

Digur nodded in agreement. "Don't banish yourself on our accounts. We can take care of ourselves."

"And each other," added Lithann.

Digur smiled and nodded again, but Inesta shook his head. "I have dedicated a large portion of my life to finding a way to erase the biggest mistake my people have ever made," he said. "My research burned up down there. I need to recreate it; I need to complete it."

Digur tried to interrupt, but Inesta pressed on. "And Jhonart was correct," he said. "The morga will continue to raid other races, abduct people, and torture them in their efforts to learn about us; to become more like us..."

He trailed off for a moment, took a deep breath, and released the air in a long, heavy sigh. "This is our fault," he said, "Our fault. We'll never admit blame, and like Digur here, I can do nothing to change the minds of my people. But I can save any poor wretches who, through no fault of their own, find themselves in the clutches of the monsters we created."

"We can stay and help you!" said Digur, and he found he meant it. "Well, I will. I cannot speak for Lithann."

"In this you can," said Lithann. "Friends stick together. This is our fight, too, now!"

"I cannot allow my friends to give up their lives for my mistakes—my sins," said Inesta. "I have done awful things in the name of the Sortilege. I must pay for those foul deeds. Call it penance. Call it justice. Perhaps one day I can join you both in Victoria. That day is simply not today."

Digur considered everything Inesta had said and nodded his head. "I understand," he said. "But before we go, teach me that trick you use to talk across great distances. Then you can call us if you ever need our help."

"Great idea," said Lithann with a huge smile that Digur thought shone brighter than the sun.

Inesta nodded. "I will teach you, but you must complete two tasks for me in return."

"Anything!" said both Digur and Lithann at the same time.

"Tell people about the danger lurking beneath our feet," said Inesta. "Again, nothing specific, and *never* mention the Sortilege. Believe me, they will hear about it and try to silence you. However, I think we all understand that defeating the morga will take a concerted effort on the part of all races. If nothing else, we must begin informing the world about the danger that lurks beneath us all."

"And the other task?" asked Digur.

"Win!" said Inesta with a smile. "Defeat all comers in Victoria. I want to hear the tales told about your victories all the way down in the dark!"

"I can't promise anything," said Digur. "But we'll try."

"Don't be silly," said Lithann, punching Digur in the shoulder. "Together, you and I can do anything we set our minds to."

With that, the three friends shook hands, hugged, cried, and said good-bye. As Inesta disappeared with a loud pop, Lithann and Digur began walking south toward Westlock, toward the city of Victoria, toward the future.

ABOUT THE AUTHOR

Will McDermott is a game writer and author. He has written for many computer games, including Guild Wars, Guild Wars 2, TERA, ZMR, and HAWKEN. Will has also written five other game-related novels—two in the Magic: the Gathering universe (Judgment and The Moons of Mirrodin), and three in the Necromunda corner of the Warhammer 40K universe (Blood Royal, Cardinal Crimson, and Lasgun Wedding). Will has raised three gamer children and lives in the Seattle area with his game designer wife and the cutest dog in the universe (whose name is not Wiley, but probably should be).

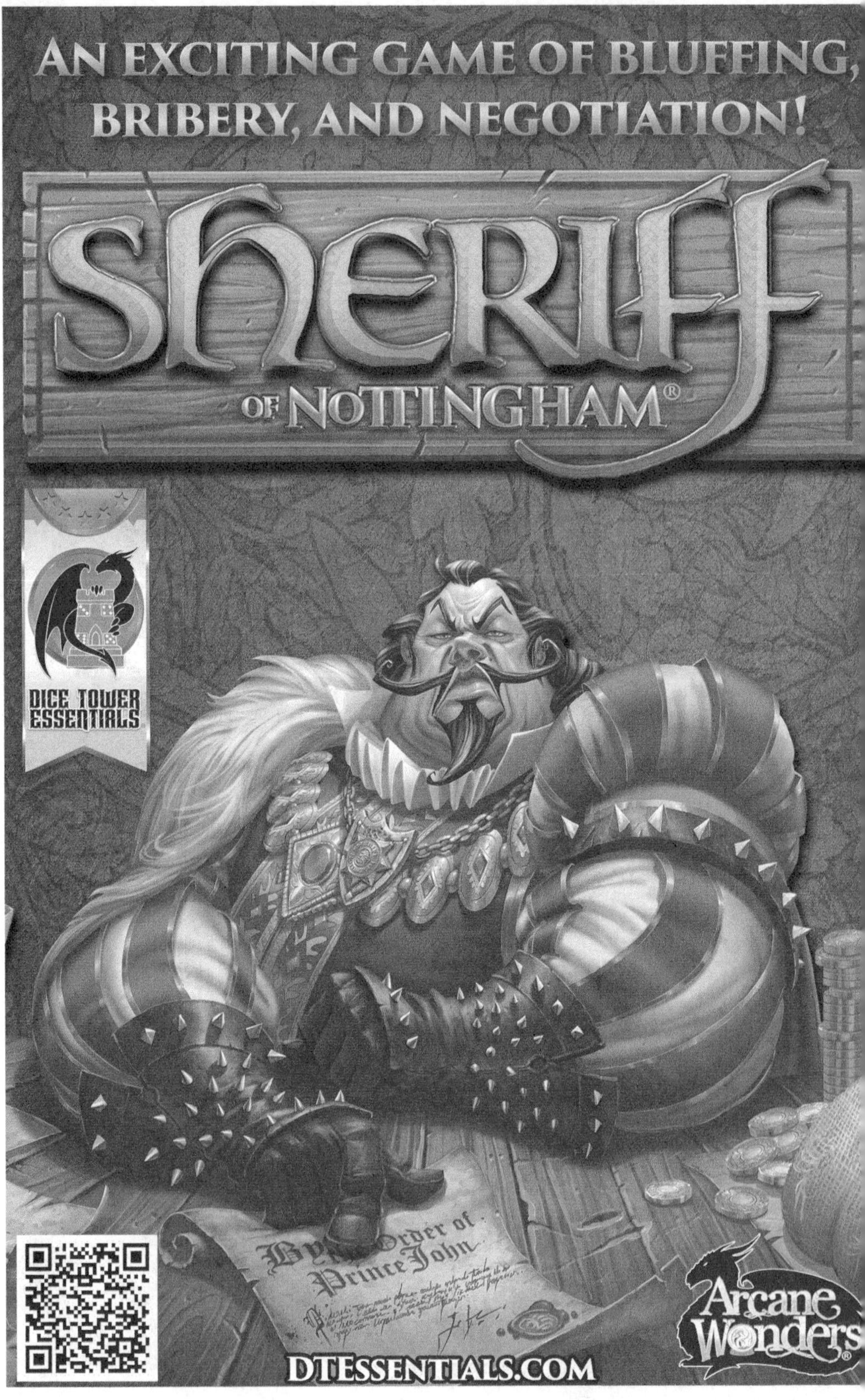
AN EXCITING GAME OF BLUFFING, BRIBERY, AND NEGOTIATION!
SHERIFF OF NOTTINGHAM®
DICE TOWER ESSENTIALS
By Order of Prince John
Arcane Wonders®
DTESSENTIALS.COM